DumpED

THE BREAKUP THAT CHANGED EVERYTHING

JENNIFER BEASLEY
LPC, CEDS

Published by hope*books
2217 Matthews Township Pkwy
Suite D302
Matthews, NC 28105
www.hopebooks.com

hope*books is a division of hope*media

Printed in the United States of America

First paperback edition.
Paperback ISBN: 979-8-89185-114-6
Hardcover ISBN: 979-8-89185-115-3
Ebook ISBN: 979-8-89185-116-0
Library of Congress Number: 2024946900

"Lia's story is one of vulnerability, courage, and, ultimately, resilience. Dump ED is a beacon of hope and understanding, providing a relatable and supportive voice for anyone struggling with an eating disorder and intricate family dynamics. It's not just a story; it's a guide for healing and self-acceptance. Dump ED is an invaluable resource for the eating disorder community and beyond."

—-Jessica Flint, M.S.

Founder & CEO of www.recoverywarriors.com

"This moving novel tells the story of a young person facing an eating disorder. It takes the reader through the struggles and courage with honesty and care. A must-read for teens, as it inspires empathy, understanding, and the importance of self-acceptance."

—Dr. Robin R. Norris, LMFT

Contents

Chapter 1

"Lia, you're up. Get to the starting line!" yells Coach Morris.

I toe the white line in the innermost lane. Four laps around the track are all I must do for this event. If I overlap the others, I know Ed will be super proud. I love it when I make him proud. Squinting into the sun-bathed stands, I can barely see my mom and older brother, but I know they are here because we drove together. My dad should be next to them, but that would be too risky for my mom's current emotional state. Since their separation, my mom completely unravels and expresses a never-ending loop of anger and sadness whenever he's around. I'm glad I don't get like that with Ed. If we ever separate, I don't know what I will do. But I don't ever want to consider this type of ending with him. I can't imagine him and I being apart. It's getting harder to remember life before meeting him, too.

The gun goes off. I start to run as fast as I can. It doesn't take long for me to hear my lungs gasping for air. I can feel the heaviness of my legs trying hard to turn over and keep up with the top half of my body. My stomach is now flip-flopping, and nausea takes the forefront. If I had eaten this morning, I would have lost it all on my new blue racing sneakers. I am grateful I double-knotted them. The crowd in the stands is loud. They are close to the track, but it sounds like they are far away. My breathing is too loud to hear any distinct cheers. Another runner in a bright orange jersey is catching up to me in the lane to my right. I can hear her quick footsteps and see her from the side of my eye. I am tempted to turn my head to see how close she is, but Coach Morris has coached me not to do this. She says it takes a second off my race time, and I need to keep my head forward and both eyes on the finish line. So, I obey. I stare straight ahead and continue to run. I need to go faster.

Two more laps to go. I can do this. I already overlapped two of the others in the outer lanes. And I surpassed the orange jersey on my right. I no longer see orange on my side or hear her Mizunos on the track. I've been told that I am fast. Most people think it's because I am training to be a collegiate runner when I leave this town in four years. But really, I get mad when I feel pain. Right now, I feel pain, and I am mad. I just want to get to the finish line and be done. The faster I run, the faster I'm done. Ed and I made up this rule together. Coach Morris has her rules; Ed and I have ours.

"Go, Lia! Don't look back! Keep running!" Coach Morris yells from the side of the track. She looks nervous. Her small frame is hunched over, and she is twisting her gray curls with her pointer finger. Doesn't she know me by now? I follow her rules. I guess I can't blame her apprehension since Ed and I have been making new rules, too. He is the one that I've been spending most of my time with since my mom and dad's fighting started last year. Don't worry, Coach Morris, I've got you! I'll get us the golden trophy. I just need to keep ignoring my chest tightening and the pain coursing through my body. I am almost done. These runs really hurt.

"You won!" cheers Coach Morris as I cross the finish line and nose-dive into the grass planted inside the track. I can't catch my breath, and my body is burning. I need to lie down for a minute.

"Lia, don't forget to properly cool down by walking the inside of the track." orders Coach Morris.

I know that I am supposed to follow her rules, but I can't. I need to lay down. Only time will tell if I can get back up. I lie in the grass and listen to the cheers of the crowd. They are welcoming the second and third-place runners. I'm too weak to see who these runners are. I wonder if the girl in the orange jersey finished or if she's coming in soon as the fourth runner. I think she went too fast in the beginning and couldn't get mad at the pain. Please don't tell anyone my secret to positive splits in a race.

Eventually, I must drag myself up and clear the track for the next event. As I walk, I try to investigate the stands. Did my mom even see my National Championship finish? Or was she too busy emotionally unraveling to my older brother, Cole, about how my dad (her soon-to-be ex-husband) should be here, too, supporting me? Even though she did not invite him nor allow me to do so. I'm starting to get used to this, though. Or, at least, I'm able to stand it a bit better without emotionally unraveling myself. I think it's because I have Ed now. I feel less alone. We met right around the time my mom and dad began fighting. My parents' summer was spent slamming doors, calling each other names, and taking turns leaving home for a few days. It took them months before my dad noticed me spending more and more time with Ed. My dad was the first one to ask about my relationship with Ed. I miss my dad. I wish he could be here today, too. I know that he would have been proud of me. Hopefully, I can see him again soon. It's been too long.

My mom says that I get my athletic talent from him. She also says my blue eyes and dirty blonde hair are his DNA. It's kind of her to share these observations with me because as time goes on, I worry I'll forget what he looks like if I don't see him soon. As usual, she can't just leave it at her complimenting the two of us.

"You know, your father really knows how to let his children down. He's always been good at that." My mom begins her typical "Your father is a loser" speech.

Normally, I would listen to her speech to avoid her repeating it if she senses my inattentiveness. But right now, I drift off and think about Ed during my mom's horrific descriptions of my dad as I escape into the girls' locker room for a moment of respite. I don't think I need to hear about how half my DNA should cease to exist for the hundredth time this month.

My brother, Cole, looks more like my mom. They both have brown hair and brown eyes. He is at the top of his class academically and wants to study law in college, like our mom. The two of them are two peas in a pod.

"Your father should have been here to see this," my mother rants as she approaches me outside the girls' locker room. I should have stayed in the bathroom stall a bit longer. Cole is busy speaking with his classmates he spotted in the crowd. I wonder if he saw me win or if he was busy building his social calendar for the rest of the weekend. Cole has a full social life. He has more friends than me and is always getting invited to go places. It's always been this way.

When I started attending high school with him, I could tell I socially disappointed him. While I will be spending my weekend cleaning our house, he will be at the movies, at the mall, etc. It seems I am the only one who cares about having a tidy home since my dad moved out.

I glimpse at the sea of people in the parking lot and see the girl in the orange jersey and Mizunos. She and her father are holding hands and walking to the mass of lined-up cars. I quickly look away and focus on looking forward. Just like I was racing. Complete blinders.

"Are you okay, Lia? We haven't seen you around as much as we used to," says Mrs. Warner, Chloe's mother.

I have known Chloe since the third grade. We have considered ourselves best friends since the day we purchased matching best friend necklaces at Claire's in the mall, the summer going into fourth grade. The kind where she got half the heart, and I got the other. Until I lost it three summers later during our family beach trip. It is somewhere in the Gulf of Mexico.

"Yeah, just been busy," I reassure her. I hope Mrs. Warner will take my short, vague response and continue walking to find her daughter, Chloe, who is somewhere in the crowd. But my mom chimes in and has found an ear to fill with her complaints about my dad not being at this national track meet.

"Jill, it is so nice to see you! Can you believe he missed such an amazing event?!"

Of course, he did; you didn't tell him about it. I hope she gets whatever emotional needs she wants met before we get in the car. Otherwise, it will be another opportunity for me to play the parent and comfort her for the whole ride home. And I am wiped.

Over the summer, my grandma called me an "old soul" for my upcoming-freshman-high-school self. Not sure what she meant by this, but I trust her ancient wisdom. It's true that I have always seemed to have more in common with adults than my peers. In elementary school, I sat with the teachers on the playground, listening to their classroom complaints, school gossip, and lesson planning instead of playing tag or climbing the monkey bars with my classmates. While they got excited about recess, I silently wished it ceased to exist. The lack of structure and loudness of it, along with the cafeteria chaos, caused me to shudder.

Ed is an old soul, too. He is very responsible and keeps me in line. While my brother is at non-parent-approved house parties, we are at my house getting ahead on homework, reading anything that is nonfiction, listening to rock music, or organizing my closet while I try to find something I want to wear on our dates. If there's time left, I will also pick up the rest of the house. For me, a clean house brings peace amid the chaos. I crave the "before" and "after" images when a room is picked up. I like evidence of my effort. I like that Ed gets this, too. He and I crave sameness, exactness, and predictability. I've noticed that others seem to get bored by this way of living, but not me. Chloe hates routines and describes them as punitive and imprisoning. Especially the ones created by her mother and father. We argue about this sometimes because she doesn't understand how much I hate surprises and why I would die of embarrassment if I ever had a surprise birthday party planned for me like she had this past year. She loved it.

The Warner family is *the* family. You know, the one that has dinner together every night around their dining room table? They take turns sharing their highs and lows from their day. They have a foreign way of being able to disagree about things without it resulting in flashing blue and red lights in their driveway with a man in uniform there to gather a report of the incident. Which is why I roll my eyes at her when she complains about her life. Seriously, her Instagram reel does not show highlights of her life but the reality of her life, and I am jealous.

I feel bad about this. Because Chloe is a great friend. "You are an amazing runner!" "You get great grades, and you don't even have to try." She likes to remind me of my natural talent in running and what a bright future I have ahead of me. She also reminds me that my honor roll academic status will soon pay off. I know her parents' inspirational and hopeful talks are speaking through her (well done, Mr. and Mrs. Warner), but it always feels so fictionalized when she talks about my options like this. I don't know where I will go to college; it will have to be a state school since it'll be up to me to cover the costs. My mom says that divorces cost a lot of money.

I'm waiting until I know where Ed plans to go. I know that I am only a freshman and not to be so concerned about these things, but escaping my home is on my mind. Regularly. This feels like a tangible path to getting out of here.

Yup, I am that girl in the neighborhood who has been riding by every evening. I choose your street, Chloe, because I know that as I pedal by, your home is filled with family and love—something I long for. As I ride by, I hope to see past the curtains and other fancy window treatments that are used to avoid the very thing I am doing: gaining an inside view into your private lives as the Warner family. A glimpse where I am a bystander and observer, without being the official guest that I have been over the years. Perhaps my longing to be included in your family is part of why the shades are left open for me to get a glimpse. I imagine it would be frightening if anyone ever discovered my intense desire to join this family. I'm always impressed by how much I learn about others from observing them in and out of their homes.

I do this at work, too. You can find me as the bag lady on cash register number four at the famous Stop & Shop of Long Island after track practice on Mondays, Tuesdays, Fridays, and most weekends. Sometimes, my manager, Mr. Pringle, will move me around, but only if another bagger doesn't show up for their assigned shift. I bag groceries for the customers.

"Do you prefer plastic, paper, or have brought your own bags?"

I've gotten pretty good at profiling each buyer and accurately guessing what they'll say before they even answer. So far, I am at 97% accuracy with a goal of getting to 100%. It helps me get through my work shifts.

I love it when Ed visits me at work. He is the 100% reusable grocery bag type of guy. He tends to be able to remember to do things like that. He is more organized and disciplined than me. I like that I know what I am getting with him. He is a keeper.

If I'm not working or hanging out with Ed or Chloe, you can find me in Matt's garage with Joey, Grace, and Sheldon. They are the opposite of Ed because they are easygoing. They have a band called "Eat at Joe's," and even though I am not a part of the band, I hang out with all of them. In middle school, I had a crush on Matt, and I was introduced to the rest of the gang after I had gathered enough nerve to hang out with Matt a few times.

We hang out. They play music and smoke marijuana. I don't. Ed would freak out if I did. He thinks that inhaling or ingesting substances weakens my self-control. He's probably right about this. The members of "Eat at Joe's" say things like, "You need to chill," "It can help you relax some," "You won't get in trouble." I smoked a few times when I wanted them to think I was worth hanging out with, but I was freaking out the entire time. It definitely did not make me feel chill or relaxed. Ed likes to remind me of these "I told you so" moments.

Chapter 2

"Get up, Lia! Or else you'll make us late again!" yells Cole from my bedroom doorway.

It must be morning time. Mornings can come too fast, and some nights, they take forever to arrive. My mornings usually start out okay when I'm still in the brief thirty seconds of leaving dreamland and landing into reality. After my arrival is when things can be good or bad. Each morning is really a game of emotional roulette. I don't know how I will feel when I wake up.

Today, I roll out of bed and slide on my blue polo shirt, navy sweatpants, and matching hoodie. One upside of Woodside High School is that it has a semi-uniform policy. This keeps my decision fatigue in the morning to a minimum. It also increases my chances of blending in with the other uniformed students at Woodside, who are also part of the blue, navy, and khaki crowds. Some days, I get by without anyone at school saying one word to me if I wear my hoodie and have my headphones on in the hallways. Those are the days I feel lucky. Having to make small talk with people is exhausting for me.

I splash cold water on my face, brush my teeth, and sloth down the stairs to the already-brewed, half-empty coffee pot. I cannot survive without my caffeine in the morning. It puts the finishing touches of fully waking up my brain waves. After my caffeine, I can begin to make sense of the environment around me. Alongside my coffee, I like to have a piece of toast with honey—just like my dad used to make for me when I was younger. I like it best served on the plate he served it on, too. It has a heart made of flowers on it. I've had it for as long as I can remember. I've never been a big fan of breakfast, but my dad used to tell me it's an important meal—which always confused me as to why my mom skips it every morning. I only like this meal when it's served on my favorite plate. It is warm and cozy (unlike my insides), and it's easy to spot in the cupboard amongst the other butter plates, salad plates, dinner plates, and saucers we've collected over the years. But this morning, it is not here. I check the dishwasher in case it has gotten behind in its daily life cycle of getting dirty, getting cleaned by the dishwasher, and then getting placed back in the cupboard.

"Did anyone take my plate? It's not where it's supposed to be!" I grunt at the top of my lungs so the whole house can stop whatever they are doing to get ready for the day and pay attention to this important matter.

"Did you check the dishwasher? And whose turn is it to unload it this morning?" my mom replies.

"I just checked. And it's not there! And no one started the wash cycle last night. Do I have to do everything around here now that Dad is gone?" I yell.

"You're doing it again, Lia! You're ruining everyone else's morning with your stupid rules. Can't use this plate, only that one. Blah, blah, blah. Just chill and think of us for a change!" Cole blurts out while coming down the stairs.

"You don't understand. I need that plate!" I snap back.

If only he knew how much I thought about him and my mom. I feel bad. I know that I am ruining everyone's morning. But if I don't stick to my beloved plate and cup, I can't bear to think about it. I have to. I have to. I have to.

I give up hope of finding my plate and settle for skipping my toast altogether and going straight for the caffeine. I'll have to grab a cup of coffee from the teachers' lounge at school when I go for my library aide shift for the first period. I got lucky getting this helping position as opposed to being a lunch aide in the cafeteria like Chloe. Hiding away in a place where talking is discouraged and I can escape in piles of books and between shelves? I credit this as being one of my top secrets to how I am surviving my freshman year of high school. I grab my backpack and a water bottle.

"I'll be waiting in the car!" I yell at Cole and my mom as I walk out and slam the front door.

I didn't mean to slam the door, but it sure feels good to do so. I hate that I am the last to wake up every morning and still the first one ready to leave the house. I hate that I could have slept for a few more minutes and did not require the abrupt waking from my brother at my doorway, only to be waiting in the car for him.

I hate that I didn't have my morning coffee and will have to wait until I get to the school grounds to fully wake my brain. But then again, maybe this is for the best. Maybe I can survive this drive to school if I'm not fully aware of the life that is happening around me. Maybe this is a good thing after all. I press the horn on the car and beep entirely too many times. I know this, but I obnoxiously continue until I see my mom and brother exit the house, flailing their arms, signaling that I need to take my hand away from the car horn. Message received, as I place my hand on my lap.

At least they finally are coming to the car. The ride to school is the same as always. My brother listens to music with headphones on and texts people he will see face-to-face in less than five minutes when we arrive at school. I listen to my latest Spotify playlist to drown out my mom's Christian radio talk. She has been trying to find healing through the words and voice of Joyce Meyer on our drives, but so far, it seems to have had no effect on her. She won't even take us to church anymore.

"Don't forget you're all taking the bus home today since I'll be working late on a case," Mom reminds us as we get out of the car at the front of our school.

"Yay, the bus. My favorite mode of transportation where I get motion sickness each ride," I reply.

Cole rolls his eyes at me because he doesn't quite get my sarcasm. I immediately scan the school grounds, looking for a friend. Someone who gets me. Someone who will help save me from the panic when I feel I do not belong in my family now that my dad is gone. But I don't see anyone I know who will understand—which only leads to the breathlessness and sweating that I try so hard not to experience outside of the track. There, it makes sense. Here, it does not.

Quick, think of the time my dad and I were playing basketball on the neighborhood courts. Think of how he would put me on his shoulders, and I got to dunk baskets like the great Michael Jordan. Now, breathe. Good, Lia. You may be able to get through this again. Keep breathing.

I walk through the doors of Woodside and duck into the library. I grab the cup of coffee that I promised myself earlier and begin shelving the books in the return pile. My sweating stops, and my breath returns to its normal rate. I make my way through the fiction section with authors' last names beginning with the letter "C."

It is here that I see Lexi and Dave kissing. They stop when they feel me staring, and Dave mumbles something about me being a stalker as they both walk off holding hands. I consider myself an observant person rather than a stalker. I was observing them kissing because I still have so much to learn. My lips feel sloppy, and I don't know what to do with my tongue most of the time. Forgive me, Lexi and Dave, for being intrigued by your display of affection towards each other.

Once again, my heart speeds up, and I begin to lose my breath. This time, I also fear that my stomach will empty the coffee onto the green rug. I grab onto the "C" shelf and breathe. I should have eaten something with it.

Quick, think of the time that my dad brought me to the library and taught me about the odd numbers on the spine of the book. I really wish the Dewey Decimal System would come back from the grave and keep my panicked mind afloat in high school. Numbers calm me. They are exact. Whatever is questionable about them, there is always an answer. Numbers are orderly and make sense to me. I especially like the even ones that can be justly shared. The odd ones sometimes trip me up, but they can still be worked with. Good—keep breathing, Lia. You've got to make it through this day.

I have a big test in English class, and I need to get an A. Getting an A gets me one step closer to earning a college scholarship, which will help me to finally be able to live a "normal" life in college. After a few minutes of thinking back to my library days with Dad, my nervous system seems to go back to homeostasis, and I now feel ready to finish my shelving duty before the bell rings to switch to my second period. Thankfully, I have Calculus class next. Calculus requires me to think in ways that are more abstract than Algebra. It requires me to commit all my attention to it. So, let the zen moments begin! Until then, shelving, breathing, and memories of my dad must keep me afloat.

The end of the first-period bell rings. I've got five minutes to get to my locker, grab my math book, and slide into the back row of Calculus. It's a test with time. I must make it before that classroom door closes. If it closes, it locks. I then have a decision to make. One: knock on the locked door and be let in by Mr. Klaus, who will ask me in front of the whole class for an explanation of why the same five minutes that allowed the other students to make it to class on time didn't allow the same for me. Then, all my classmates will stare at me, and I may even hear whispers and snickers as I walk to find an empty desk to sink into and pray I might disappear.

Or two: I can try to avoid that huge level of embarrassment and skip the class entirely, but then lose my perfect attendance record for the year while also feeling guilty about missing the lecture and assignment. Both options aren't real options for me. So, making it to Mr. Klaus's classroom door before it closes is my only option.

I never anticipated having to factor into my five-minute relay what I would do if I saw Ed with another girl. And there they are. They are standing at the locker right next to mine. And she is beautiful. She has long brown hair and blue eyes. She is smiling, and her perfectly straight and whitened teeth are displayed for all of us to admire. She is dressed in our semi-uniform of a navy polo and khaki skirt, but she wears them like a J. Crew catalog model. Maybe she is one? I haven't seen her here before. Maybe she is new? I don't know. But what I do know is that I do not like seeing Ed with her.

Maybe she is just a new girl, and he is showing her to her class? That's kind of him. Or maybe she is his cousin who he never told me about who is visiting? I hope he introduces me. Whichever it is, I'm sure it will be okay. Then why does my stomach feel like it's eating itself again? I look away. Within seconds, I peek back to the locker. She's gone. He's gone. Where did they go? I don't have time for this. I need to get to Mr. Klaus's classroom before the bell rings again.

Just like that, I grab the doorknob as Mr. Klaus is pulling the other side of it shut. I give him a quick smile and walk to the empty desk in the back row. As I sit down, I make sure to thank God above for having time on my side today. The blue plastic seat feels extra hard and cold today, even with my sweatpants on. Do they make these chairs so uncomfortable to keep students from falling asleep in class? If so, their scheme isn't working because, to my left, Darius is now drifting off into dreamland. Are the desk chairs so hard to keep students from bouncing on them? Again, if so, their scheme isn't working. Kari is bouncing her legs so fast to my right that I'll be smelling rubber from her sneaker bottoms any minute now. Her leg bouncing is so irritating!

Focus, Lia. It's math time. I like math, remember? I take out a sharpened pencil and my spiral notebook labeled Calculus. I like the college-ruled notebooks instead of wide-ruled ones. I imagine this moves me closer to my college readiness goals. I also prefer newly sharpened pencils. I am happy with myself for remembering to use the electric pencil sharpener in the library before classes began for the day. For Calculus, I use my pencil that has a good eraser in case I make a mistake. I rarely do because math is one of my best classes, but just in case.

I try to pay attention to Mr. Klaus, but thoughts of Ed begin to take over. Where did he go, and when will I see him again? I know we have just recently gotten more serious, but I didn't realize how much I hate seeing him with someone else. I want him here with me.

Chapter 3

*I*t is rare, but sometimes, life can be on my side. Since last week in Mr. Klaus's class, when I was pining for Ed but was supposed to be calculating and processing the numbers that Mr. Klaus was spewing out to our class, I've been able to spend more time with Ed. And I really needed more time with him since I've been receiving more attention from people at school. Earlier this week, on the school news, they shared that our school won the gold trophy at the National Track Championship, which will now be displayed in a glass case in front of the school gym. I like to run, and I like to win. But I do not like drawing attention to myself. This is an equation I have not been able to solve just yet. Can you see why I really like math now? Facing equations that are solvable!

My mom and Cole have not met Ed yet. Honestly, I don't plan to have them meet him any time soon. A part of me wants to keep him all to myself and have him see me for who I really am rather than how my mom and Cole see me. I love them. I really do. And there are times when I connect with them, but these times are sparse and brief. I don't know why I feel so much like an outsider inside my home. I try to think back on if it's always been this way, and it seems it has. It wasn't as apparent when my dad was here because I feel like he and I are a lot more alike. But now that he is absent, it feels like I am sinking into the big hole of absence that he gifted us all with. Like my garage band friends from "Eat at Joe's," I am not sure my mom and sisters will like Ed because he's different.

Does my dad think of us? Does he miss us? Why didn't he and my mom go to couples counseling and try to work it out? Last month, when I was at my grandma's house, Oprah was on the TV. That afternoon, she was interviewing a married couple who had almost divorced after the husband had an affair. When the wife found out, she shared how she was hurt and filed for divorce. Both she and her husband shared their story. I was doing my homework and not fully listening to all the details, but it sounded like couples counseling really worked for them, and they decided to stay married. I wish Mom and Dad would have been willing to give couples counseling a try.

Are Cole and I not worth trying to stay together for? Was it terrible for the four of us to be an intact family? I really don't understand what my mom and dad's fights were about. I just know they escalated fast and were scary. There were times I hid in my closet, hoping the clothing and sliding doors would block out some of their name-calling and yelling. At some point, dishes were thrown at the wall and fell shattered on the wooden floor. Cole would escape to his room, put headphones on, and blast music. It wouldn't end until one of them would leave, slamming the front door so hard it shook the house. But I am older now and more prepared because I have Ed. I don't think they would be as scary for me now. I think my dad should come back home. I can handle their fights better this time around. I can just leave when they start.

I like that my grandma and grandpa live close to us. I can get to their house within ten minutes on my bike. No major roads to cross, and my grandma is almost always home. Their home is comforting for me. My grandma keeps it clean and tidy. It has a distinct smell to it that reminds me of coffee and toast, blended with a whiff of my grandpa's Old Spice aftershave and cologne that he gets gifted to him for Christmas every year by my mom. He is a coin collector. He has coin collector albums consistently stacked on their dining room table. His coins are meticulously sorted by years. He constantly searches for the last coin of a collection. He picks up the pennies we often walk by in the Stop & Shop parking lot in hopes that a newfound treasure has arrived at his feet. He continues to show up to work each workday, and I don't think he ever plans to retire. He says that work gives him purpose and structure.

My grandparents have been married for over fifty years. They do argue, but their arguments do not result in a uniformed man stepping out of a white car with flashing blue and red lights. Their fights aren't scary to me. They feel tolerable.

My grandparents regularly tell me that they don't like my dad. When they say these things, I feel a heavy brick in my stomach, a large lump in my throat, and a stream of tears waiting to spill over my eyes and run down my cheeks. They chose the side of my mom (their daughter) when it came to having to pick a side. I am trying to stay neutral for as long as possible because I don't want to pick a side. But because my mom already has my brother and her two parents on her side, I feel I should be on my dad's side so he won't be alone. This seems like the right thing to do.

So far today, I've completed six of the ten chores that I need to finish before I get to spend the evening with Ed. This morning, when I transitioned from dreamland to reality, the emotional roulette came to rest in it being a good day for me. I have begun to learn how important it is to do what needs to be done on these good days. With each new sunrise, the emotional roulette begins to spin, and I do not know on which side all bets will land. Will it be a good day or a bad day?

Before I met Ed, bad days were hopeless. Since being with him, things are more tolerable, and I can get through the bad days without wanting to disappear completely. Breathe, Lia. Think of the many mornings that Dad would make us breakfast before school. The time I had mini bagels with a smear of my favorite whipped cream cheese for the eyes and the perfectly ripe, curvy banana for the mouth. Remember that smiley face cuisine he served? Remember how much he knew my likes and dislikes? Remember how he would encourage me to try new foods when I wasn't sure of them? This ensured a good day. It's been a while since I tried something new. It's been a while since Dad has been here. Now, take this image into the rest of the day, and chances are my day will remain good. Even better, if my plate with a heart made of flowers on it, is returned to the cupboard before tomorrow morning, the chances of two good days in a row will increase drastically.

"I'm going to the office to work more on a case, Lia. I left money on the table for you and Cole to order a pizza," my mom shouts from downstairs.

"Okay," I yell from upstairs.

I tend to relate better to my mom when communicating from another room. It seems to work better for both of us. Cole is out and about as any other high schooler would be on this Friday night. So, the twenty-dollar bill left for pizza is all mine. I run downstairs to get it and stash it away with the other Harriet Tubman portraits of currency. I have squirreled these away from numerous Friday night dinners that I have not ordered. I am saving them up to buy my first car. My grocery bagging job provides, but not at the rate I need it to. If I am going to realistically survive these next four years of high school without my dad, I need some form of transportation to escape my ordinary life. Nothing fancy, just something with good gas mileage and four working tires that can get me to school, work, coffee shops to attend open mic nights, and Matt's garage to hang out with him and the others. Ed always seems to find me, which I love, but I'd also like to make more of an effort to find him, too.

Time to throw another load of laundry in the dryer and fold the warm articles that just finished their drying cycle. The towels feel so toasty and warm me up as I carry them to the cold leather couch to begin my folding. The leaves on the trees in our yard are beginning to change colors, and sweater weather has begun. Lately, however, I have felt chillier than usual for this time of year, which is weird due to the global warming we are experiencing. Ed says not to worry too much about it because he will be sure to find ways to keep me warm. Isn't that sweet of him? Always trying to find a solution for me.

Tonight, we are going to watch a movie together, and I cannot wait. He likes psychological thrillers since those are the only ones that can keep his interest. Other less intense movies leave him talking to me throughout the whole thing, and I miss most of the movie! It can be annoying. I like comedies, but I usually let Ed decide what we will watch. We used to take turns picking, but then I realized if we don't watch his movie, my movie is pretty much trash because of his constant interruptions. To me, it makes most sense to just let him choose.

The same goes for the snacks that we have for movie nights. When Ed and I first met, my mom and dad would watch the movies with us. My dad and Ed used to join me in eating popcorn and chocolate-covered raisins, a mix I introduced them both to. The best of both worlds, sweet and salty. But when my dad moved out, and mom got busy dating again, it was just me and Ed for movie nights. He started telling me that we should just stick to one of those, and whenever I made both, he left one of them untouched, which felt like a waste to me. It also made me feel super awkward to eat it in front of him and have him watch me with a disapproving look. So, I started to wait until he arrives to make snacks, and he usually turns them down. I guess it's one less thing for me to fret about, but I do miss the popcorn and chocolate-covered raisin mix I used to make.

One time, I made my mix and ate it before he arrived. I thought I was clever and ate what I enjoyed before he arrived. But not clever enough because his nose turned up when he entered the house, and his judgmental look crushed me. Things were distant between us that night. I won't make that mistake again.

I quickly finish folding the clothes and piling them in each of my family members' designated piles. I no longer fold my mom's clothes, as most of hers need to be dropped off and picked up at the dry cleaners. She is a litigation lawyer and prefers her court attire to be perfectly pressed. I've also noticed her business suit sizes vary throughout the year. She tends to jump from the newest fad diet to the next in an attempt to get smaller. It is ridiculous to watch her go a week only eating cabbage or a week only eating butter and meat. She claims she needs to be healthier but does the most absurd, unhealthy things. I am confused.

She is also a bit peculiar about the way her pajamas are cared for, so I am always sure to fold them tightly right out of the dryer so they do not wrinkle. I put her clothes away first, in her drawer, to be sure they are where they need to be when she needs them. Next, I fold and bring Cole's clothing upstairs to his room. Cole has a cool and unique style. He is older than me and way cooler than me. Truthfully, there are times I deeply question if there is a coolness gene that I just don't have.

Cole is the type of kid that you cannot place in one social circle. He's involved with the theater club, on the school soccer team, and is one of the most popular juniors at the school. He is running for class president and will most likely win—even more evidence that supports my theory of how much cooler he is than me.

Ouch, another stabbing headache. I've been getting these more regularly. They start with an annoying thump, which then turns into a mean ice pick beating inside my head if I choose to ignore the thumping and instead continue with my hustling of the day. When I searched WebMD for what the cause could be, its response was anything between a brain aneurysm that requires immediate medical attention, to me needing to increase my water intake. It's hard to know what level of severity my headache will fall each time. My recent ones did not get better with increasing my hydration, but did resolve after I ate dinner and slept them off.

Maybe today's headache is brought to me by the pressure of feeling everyone's stares on me at school all day after our team brought back the trophy for the school. Or maybe it was the pain I felt that struck me when I saw that my mom's closet is empty on one side where my dad's belongings once hung. Or maybe it is the beginning of a hemorrhage in my brain. I do not know. All I know is that the laundry will have to wait. I'm calling Ed to cancel. I need to lay down or die, whichever one comes first.

Chapter 4

"Chloe!" I yell.

All the hallways at school resemble a long tunnel for me. A tunnel with no light at the end, except for when I get to exit the building at the end of each day after dismissal. Each hall is lined with navy blue lockers on both sides of the hall. In between sections of them is a classroom door. I know that I had to yell to ensure my voice would reach her, but I hope none of the other students can hear me, just Chloe. As usual, what I hoped would happen does not. Completely typical when it comes to my life. All the students, except for Chloe and those with headphones on, turn to look at me yelling down the hall trying to get my best friend's attention. I really despise eyes looking at me. And she doesn't stop. Chloe continues to walk down the long, noisy tunnel, the freshman hallway.

I bet she is reciting her lines for the school play in her head and can't hear me. Sometimes, Cole does this for his drama club, and I have to call his name many times before he responds to my existence. I'll just have to text Chloe instead. I've been meaning to do this anyway. I am beginning to feel like a bad friend for not hanging out with her as much as I had before school started. Even worse, I have not been texting her back like I usually do. I have been leaving her texts on read for the last several weeks. I'm not upset with her or trying to ignore her. I am annoyed with the whole world spinning and existing around me.

And my quick-onset, constant headaches aren't helping. I have been avoiding Ed more because of them. He keeps wanting me to do things, and I haven't had the enthusiasm or ability to do them like I had a couple of weeks ago. I feel like I am stuck in slow motion. Brushing my teeth feels like twenty steps instead of just brushing and rinsing. Up until last month, I would brush my teeth twice a day, floss, and whiten. Now, my pearly whites are lucky if they get brushed once every two days. When making decisions, my mind ping-pongs before finally landing on something. Each day, when deciding what to pack for lunch, I've had to narrow the choices down to two: peanut butter on wheat bread or carrots and hummus. Adding any other option to the ping pong match would just completely overwhelm me. Having the same things is easier for me. I started to pack my lunch to prevent any unneeded surprises. The school lunch menu will say one thing, and the cafeteria staff will serve another. This kind of inconsistency makes my skin crawl. I feel every goose bump covering my arms and legs, and it makes me want to scream. To avoid these school cafeteria shout outs, I bring my bagged lunch.

Besides, packing my lunch allows me to eat with Ed in the rows of titles and authors in the library. The smell of book pages and coffee from the teachers' lounge fills the air. There are round tables used for reading, writing, and studying. I know the library rules are no eating and drinking, but I am careful when I do both. I sit in between the aisles of history books on the green carpet and take small bites, being sure not to draw the attention of others. Some days, I just forgo the whole ordeal and read with Ed. This is my favorite way to spend my lunch hour. I wish I could just become a bear in need of a long winter hibernation. This would be helpful for me to get through life as of late.

"Lia, can you come to my office for a moment, please?" The school counselor pulls me back to the high school halls and away from the comfy hibernation cave I am daydreaming of.

"Sure," I fake agree, even though every part of me wants to run to my usual routine as a library aide this period. I find peace in the process of reshelving the variety of titles and authors that my peers read. Instead, I obediently follow Ms. Amy to her office.

I wonder if this has to do with me winning the massive gold trophy that's being displayed in the school's glass case. I really hope this is not a personal recognition and congratulations for my running performance that helped bring this trophy here. I don't do well with receiving attention. My heart beats fast, my breathing speeds up, and my eyes get cloudy. The attention makes me want to squirm out of my skin, like a snake shedding.

"Have a seat wherever you feel most comfortable." Ms. Amy invites me into her office space, also coined the school's "safe place."

I scan our "safe place" and silently vote for which seat looks the comfiest. The solo oversized brown lounge chair will do. Ms. Amy will probably sit at her desk, but just in case she doesn't, my personal space won't be at risk of being invaded like it would if I choose the three-person orange couch. I have a low risk tolerance.

"Do you know why you are here, Lia?" quizzes Ms. Amy.

"I have no idea." Little does Ms. Amy know that my insides are begging for an answer. I do not like surprises, the unknown, and uncertainty. They cause me to sweat and breathe hard like I am running a race on the track, but instead, I am sitting in this "safe place." I really hope she does not leave me hanging in suspicion much longer. I sit in the chair with my arms crossed. I have a feeling I need my shield.

"Okay. Well, Coach Morris and your good friend, Chloe, have come to me separately to voice their concerns about you not attending lunch hour like you used to. They also shared that you appear to be pulling away from your classmates and have had less energy than usual. What do you think of their concerns?"

"Um, I'm not sure what they're referring to." I am annoyed. What nerve of Chloe and Coach Morris to talk about me behind my back to Ms. Amy. It's no wonder Chloe dodged me in the halls just before I was pulled into this interrogation. She probably wasn't ready to see how mad I am with her right now. I despise pop-up conversations of any kind, but especially ones like this.

"How are things at home?"

"Good."

What I really want to say is that things are not good. My mom has constant worry, which seeps into the nervous systems of the rest of us in the house, even when we don't want it to. My dad is supposed to be visiting with me and my sisters every weekend, according to the custody agreement, but that isn't happening. Cole is the star of the high school musical, well-liked by everyone, and does not seem very affected by things like me. It seems his soul has a Teflon barrier where negativity just doesn't stick. He is running for class president and making major moves in the student council of our school, and he flirts with every cute girl because they all want his attention. As for me? I just want to disappear with Ed.

I also want Ms. Amy to know that if she ever needs to talk to me again, can she please not pull me out of my first period of being a library aide? The library is my cave. I need to hibernate there before entering the halls of this high school for the rest of the day. I really hope she is reading my mind now, only for this thought. Then, exit her mind-reading abilities to keep all my other thoughts private, solely for me.

"How are things at school?"

"Fine."

Again, what I really want to say is my longtime friend, Chloe, betrayed me by speaking to you. My coach, who I won a trophy for, betrayed me by speaking to you. I will remember not to give the extra effort next track season- if I even join the team after this. And my few friends from the garage band are in all different classes from me this year since I've been assigned to AP classes. I rarely see them. And I don't go to the cafeteria because I don't know anyone there, and I feel like I'd be putting myself at risk to be hunted by the various lunch table cliques I read about that occur in high school cafeterias. No, thank you.

"Okay, well, please know that I am here for you if you ever want to talk." Ms. Amy says in closing.

"Thank you."

Again, what I really want to say is, please leave me alone and pretend that this awkward interaction didn't happen and just let me get through my freshman year unnoticed.

"Can I go to first period now?" I ask, holding my breath, hoping no more questions will be fired in my direction. I don't know if I can handle being shot my way.

"Yes, you can. Please come by if you need anything." She states.

Phew, I thought I was going to pass out after holding my breath, waiting for her to answer. Luckily, her statement ended with a period and not a question mark. The end. Time to get to my cave in the library, where I can recover and find peace in shelving the returned books in their proper places. I help them find their homes when they are misplaced.

"Lia, Lia? Are you okay? Wake up." Ms. Amy requests of me as I lay on the ground of her office doorway. I am halfway out and half in. I was so close to escaping. Why did my body betray me at a time like this? This makes three betrayals for today, and it's still just the first period.

"Yeah, I think I just got up too fast," I mumble as I sit up quickly to convince her, my actions backing up my words. But I think I stood up too fast. It's getting dark again.

Chapter 5

"You are in the emergency room at a children's hospital. You passed out at school and had to be brought here by ambulance. Do you know your name?" asks a woman dressed in white scrubs with Disney characters all over them.

Too bad this isn't just a bad ride at Magical Kingdom.

"Um, yes. My name is Lia Llyod." I answer quietly.

Did anyone see me get carried away by the ambulance? That would be humiliating. How could my body betray me like this? I have never passed out before. Why did it choose high school, of all places, to begin doing so?

"Correct. Do you know how old you are?"

"Yes, I just turned fifteen. Does anyone else know that I am here?"

"Correct. Your mother and father have both been called."

Great. Both Mom and Dad have been brought into this embarrassing situation. As if I needed more evidence of being the odd one of the family. The one who made a dramatic scene at school.

"Why don't you get some rest? I will be back shortly to take your vitals again. The remote for the television is to your right, and the nurse call button is on the remote. Let me know if you need anything."

The nurse, disguised as a Disney tour guide, leaves the room. Leaving me with the bright fluorescent lights, a beeping machine that matches my heart rhythm, a bunch of wires taped to my body, and a television in the corner. I have no idea what time it is. I'm relieved that the nurse didn't quiz me on that. I would have failed, and perhaps a CT scan of my brain would have been ordered. I hope I don't have to have one. On the Discovery Channel, I watched someone go into that machine, and it looked like a live person being put into a coffin—but instead of silence and peace of the world, six feet under, the CT scanning device lets out loud bangs and buzzes that echo within the smallest, most confined space a live human could ever be succumbed to.

Just as I begin to get lost in my imagination of being rolled away to the CT scanning room, Ed saves the day. Thank you, Ed. He always seems to know when I need him the most. He will help me make sense of this debacle. Did I not drink enough water? Did I forget to eat breakfast again? What caused my body to force me to the ground to allow my blood to rush to my head, eventually allowing me to wake? That's another thing I learned on Discovery Channel: how your body smartly knows when it needs more blood flow to the brain, which causes you to lose consciousness and fall.

When you have fallen, the brain gets its way. It gets the blood it so desperately needs. It's a smart system, the human body. But I think my brain demands too much blood and should learn to find another method that won't ruin my high school reputation.

"Lia, I'm Dr. Whittaker. I will be taking care of you along with Nurse Joyce. How are you feeling?" Asks a man in his thirties who has unluckily balded much too young. I'm also guessing Nurse Joyce is the Disney World tour guide whom I met earlier.

"I'm okay. And you?" I answer in my most cheery tone to paint the picture that I am doing great. Discharge me now. I assume he needs to witness something before handing me the highly valuable discharge papers—the key to getting unplugged from these devices and exiting through the double doors that lead to the parking lot, where my getaway car is waiting somewhere.

"Thanks for asking. Honestly, I am concerned about you. Is this the first time you've passed out?"

"Yes,." I lie. The fact is, it is not. I passed out a few times last month. This is just the first time I've been caught. Technically, I am not fully lying to Dr. Whittaker. Loopholes—you've got to love them.

"Okay. Do you remember how you were feeling before you passed out?"

"Fine. I guess I was a bit annoyed that I was missing my favorite period of the school day as the library aide because Ms. Amy called me into her office. But other than that, fine."

"Okay. Well, I'm going to have you change into this gown; it opens in the back. I will be back in a bit. If you have any questions, Nurse Joyce is near."

"Okay. Thank you."

As the friendly, bald young doctor leaves, I begin to change into the gown. It's probably best at this point to follow all the instructions of the gatekeeper who holds my discharge papers. The gown is yellow with zoo animals. They are cute. But I feel a bit elementary for my high school self. I tie the hospital gown with the opening in the back, as instructed, which leaves me feeling more exposed than ever. You can be certain you will never find me on Gunnison Beach in my lifetime.

"Do you need any help?" Disney World tour guide (aka Nurse Joyce) asks from behind the privacy curtain.

"No, I've got it. Do you know when I can go home?"

"I'm not sure. I know the doctor is ordering some tests first to be sure you are okay."

Tests?! I say a quick prayer in my mind: Dear God, I know I have been a bit absent from you since being busy with Ed and school and work and life in general. But I am here now, begging you to please not let me be placed in that coffin of a CT scan. I promise to pray more. Amen.

Disney World tour guide pulls the privacy curtain away with the biggest smile, like she had just heard that the line to Space Mountain has no wait on the busiest day at the park. She places an apple juice in a little clear container with a foil top. If I had not read the foil top stating it was apple juice, I would have easily mistaken it for a urine sample. Alongside it is a pack of graham crackers.

"The doctor said it's okay to get you something to eat and drink before the tests."

No need to waste your resources on me. I most likely won't touch them because my stomach is doing flips and twists, and eating seems hard to incorporate into my intestinal gymnastics routine. It seems since knowing Ed, my stomach has not been itself. I suppose this is what butterflies in the stomach feel like, that some people speak of when they are in love.

I have never been in love before. I have never relied on someone other than my parents to support me. My mom is available sometimes; other times, she says she can't handle the things I come to her with, hoping I'll receive comfort and a hug by doing so. Sometimes, I do; other times, I end up providing her with comfort. My dad was able to give me a pep talk or let me know how to go about problem-solving whatever puzzling situation I was in. But since the separation, which is resulting in a final divorce, my dad has not been a viable option.

"Oh my gosh, Lia, are you okay?" Chloe bursts through the privacy curtain at full speed, like the first-place runner would burst through the finish line ribbon of a marathon.

"Not really. Why did you betray me to Ms. Amy?" I grudgingly force myself to answer her since my curiosity for her answer is stronger than my disappointment in her.

"Because I have been worried about you. I didn't know how to tell you."

"You could have just told me instead of talking about me behind my back!"

"I know that I should have, but you have been shrinking away since the beginning of summer. And avoiding me. It's like you're suddenly too cool to hang out with me."

"Yeah, that's what kids do! We change before entering high school. Seriously, Chloe!"

I quickly rewind to the beginning of summer until now, scanning my memories for what possibly could have given Chloe this idea. I attended tennis camp as usual. My family canceled our Hamptons beach trip because Cole got sick. I began getting to know Ed better since we started hanging out more. I rode my bike regularly to my grandparents' house and spent some time in their swimming pool. Perhaps I hadn't made enough time to hang out with her as she would've liked. Whatever. That doesn't justify speaking to the school counselor behind my back.

"But you haven't been acting like yourself."

"My dad is gone, Chloe. My mom has been doing worse since then. Of course, you wouldn't understand since you have a perfect family."

"That's not fair to say, Lia. I'm leaving!" And just like that, she blows through the privacy curtain again and stomps off.

It really is a good thing she left; I don't need this stress or anything else spiking my blood pressure, my heart rate, or my respiratory rate—which are all difficult to hide when I have machines beeping because of this spike. Thanks, Chloe. Way to get the nurses' concern, which is the exact opposite of my plan to get out of here. I really don't know when our friendship went from being connected at the neck by best friend charms to being further away than ever.

"Lia, we are going to draw some blood. Do you prefer a certain arm?" Nurse Joyce asks me with a little too much excitement about drawing blood from my body.

"Either arm is fine," I mumble.

"It should just hurt for a second," she blatantly lies because it hurts the whole time.

"I am going to send these samples to the lab, and the doctor will be back to discuss the results once your parents arrive."

"Good luck getting them both to come and be okay being in the same building as each other," I blurt out and quickly regret disclosing too much about my family to this stranger. Ed is really the only one outside the family unit who knows these things. Why can't I control what comes out of my mouth? And just like that, as though my mom's ears heard me sharing family secrets, she walks in the room to repair the family image just in time—with a smile on her face and dressed in her professional lawyer attire of a gray business pants suit with a white buttoned blouse peeking through.

"Lia, what happened?" she asks, with more curiosity than the worried tone you'd expect from a parent walking into a hospital room to see their child strapped to cords and machines.

"I don't know, Mom. But I'm sure I am fine," I reply reassuringly, which is really a mother's role in this situation.

"Okay. Well, I will be in the hall finishing up my work call. Have the doctor come get me when they arrive, please?"

"Sure," I whisper.

Whatever, Mom. Your child is in the hospital, and your legal work is your focus. Got it. Nothing really changes. But at least you are consistent; I'll give you that. Maybe next time, you can at least pretend you are concerned about me.

"Lia, I'm here. What happened to you?" My dad briskly runs through the privacy curtain and is at the side of my bed. He looks concerned, just as a father should be. He's always had the best bed-side manner.

"I don't really know. I just woke up here. The nurse and doctor haven't told me anything yet." I speak softly.

I look up at him and cannot stand to see the sadness in his eyes. I want to ask him why he hasn't been around on the weekends like he promised he would be at the beginning of the separation. I want to ask him if he misses me and Cole. I want to know where he sleeps every night now that he's not home. I want to know if he is happy, sad, mad, or all of the above. But I don't want to upset him because then he will leave, and I really like seeing him.

"Mom is here. She's on a call for work but should be back soon." I offer up some conversation to keep myself from asking my questions.

"Of course she is. That woman is always working, isn't she? Even in this incident, she won't take a break. She will never change!" My dad angrily states.

Oh no, am I making him mad? If he's mad, he may leave. I don't want him to.

"It's okay, Dad. I'm fine. I'm sure it's a big case, or else she would." I defend my mom against his harsh judgment. I've got to contain their feelings to keep them under the same roof of this hospital long enough for me to figure out what is happening to me. Ed would have come by already but is concerned the hospital staff and my parents will disapprove of him. He's not liked by most parents, he once told me. I get it. So, we decided he will come back after I leave the emergency room.

"Sure. Okay. How are you feeling, honey?" He pulls a chair close to the bedside and leans in as he speaks. I can smell the canned tuna mixed with pickles and onions that he had for lunch. Strangely, that smell brings me comfort in having him nearby. He has eaten the same workday lunch every day for as long as I can remember. He packs it on ice in his red cooler, along with various other items that do differ from day to day. He works in commercial construction, and his job is labor-intensive. He hurt his back last year, so he has been considering changing careers, but as of now, he has not.

"I'm okay. Ready to go home, though," I reply.

"I bet. Let's see what the doctor says. Let me go see if I can spot him in the hallway." He gets up and walks through the privacy curtain, leaving the room.

After a few minutes of beeping machines, footsteps up and down the hall, and chattering coming from the nurses' station, I hear my mom and dad speaking with Dr. Whittaker. I get out of bed and lean toward the privacy curtain to hear better. I am relieved that both my mom and dad are speaking at a normal volume instead of yelling at each other. I can't quite hear what they are saying, but I do hear the doctor.

"We ran some blood tests, and your daughter's iron is low, white blood cells are low, and so are her potassium levels. I've noticed her frail frame, and she reports her menstrual cycle has stopped over the summer. With all of this, I suspect that your daughter will benefit from a full psychiatric evaluation with our psych provider, Dr. Cramer, on the sixth floor. If you give me permission for Lia to be evaluated, I can get him down here this evening." Dr. Whittaker strongly suggests.

"Yes, whatever you think she needs," quickly gasps my mom.

"I agree," says my dad.

What?! Did I just witness my parents agreeing with each other? WOW. At least something good is coming from this nightmare of a day. But seriously, a psych evaluation? Why would they agree to that? I'm not crazy. I just fainted. My mom's sobbing surely gave away whatever discretion Dr. Whittaker and his nurse had hoped for. In truth, I heard the entire conversation happening in the hospital hallway outside of this room they have me stashed away in. Now I must find a way to be sure Dr. Cramer will see how sane I am.

"Lia, they want to do another test." My dad shares as he walks through the privacy curtain again. Not sure how much privacy this really allows.

"I know. I know. You all think I am crazy. I heard it all." I quickly reply to save him from having to lie to my face about what test is left.

I need to believe he is on my side. Regardless of him no longer keeping his end of the weekend visits up recently. I know he must be on my side and know that I am not crazy.

"No. But talking to someone couldn't hurt, right?" asks my dad.

"Fine! But then, can I please leave this place?" I plead. I cannot take the bright fluorescent lights, the ice-cold air conditioner, this tissue paper thin gown with an exposed backside, and the beeping of the machines. I need to go.

"Why don't you try eating something before the next test? What can I bring you from the cafeteria?" my dad offers.

"I'm not hungry. Maybe a coffee and an apple?" I request.

"Sure." he answers as he walks through the privacy curtain again.

After he leaves, all I can think about is how to spend more time with Ed. He always seems to help me. I don't want to share him with my parents, especially after they agreed to have me be seen by the psych provider. I bet they think I am crazy for liking someone like Ed. He's probably not who they pictured me to be with. But what do they know about relationships? Theirs ended terribly.

Chapter 6

"Honey, I can't believe this is happening," my mom sobs as she enters the room and pulls the privacy curtain to the wall. So much for privacy. Figures. My mom has never been one to respect my privacy, which is why I don't tell her about Ed. The whole block, neighborhood, town, state, and country would know about me and him within hours.

"What is happening, Mom?"

"You are sick. You need help." She explains through her sobbing.

"I'm fine, Mom."

"What happened? Was it your father and I separating? Am I a terrible mother?" She continues mumbling in between tears and blowing her nose. She takes out her mirror from her purse and begins to reapply her mascara and powder. No matter what the day brings, she always comes prepared with her purse of makeup, medication she takes to calm her anxiety, and her mirror. I suppose her wallet, keys, and phone are somewhere in there, too. She pops a pill and swallows hard. I look past her theatrics and see nurses walking the halls. I see a young boy about eight years old being wheeled in a wheelchair back to his room across the hall. I can't see much else through his privacy curtain. But it looks as though others are waiting for him on the other side because there are two pairs of shoes peeping under the curtain. Adult-sized shoes. One is a women's pair. The other is a men's pair. I suspect they belong to his mother and father. How nice for them to be sitting in the same room as each other. Side by side.

"Here's your apple and coffee, Lia. I had them put cream and sugar in it, too," my dad proudly announces as he enters and hands me the styrofoam cup.

I grab it and am instantly irritated. First, how could he ask for those add-ons? Doesn't he know that I drink my coffee black since meeting Ed? Second, doesn't he know my thoughts on styrofoam and how terrible it is for our environment? He would if he came around more.

"Thanks," I mumble through gritted teeth and quickly plan to hold the cup to warm up, not actually consume it.

And for the apple—well, it's my attempt at gaining some luck. Haven't you heard of the association between apple consumption and doctor visits?

"Why didn't you bring her an actual meal, David?" my mom snuffs at my dad's delivery.

"Because this is all she wanted, Julia!" snarks my dad.

"I'm fine, guys," I interrupt the start of a potential verbal war. At least they are using each other's names instead of the obscene ones they usually use when referring to each other.

"Hello. I'm Dr. Cramer. Lia, it's so nice to meet you," a short man with bifocals reaches out his hand to shake mine.

"Hello," I reply, shaking his hand. I am thankful for this help in interrupting the parental war that was about to begin.

"Your hands are so cold. Are they always this cold?" he asks.

I shrug my shoulders. Truthfully, I've heard this before from Chloe, but I won't share this unnecessary added information with him.

"Mr. and Mrs. Lloyd, is it possible for you two to join us for the first portion of the evaluation and then step out for the remaining?" he politely asks.

I like that he refers to them both as a married couple. Does he know he just interrupted a potential verbal warfare between the two? Probably not. Probably best to keep him unaware of how he stepped into their crossfire. It will be entertaining to see how he responds. Most don't do well. I have survived it because I know where the emotional landmines are between the two, and I stay away from them. But it took me fourteen years to feel partially equipped for this event.

"Sure," they say simultaneously. What world am I living in where they once again agree without hesitation? I missed this.

"How do you think Lia is doing with sleeping, self-hygiene, and eating?" he asks the room.

"I don't think she's having any problems with those things. She loves to sleep, and it is hard to wake her in the morning to get ready for school, but once she's up, she gets ready. Her brother is really into doing his hair—you know, making himself present-able before leaving the house—but Lia has never shown interest in those things. We haven't been eating together much lately due to a big case at work, her father having recently moved out, and her brother being busy at his friends' houses. So, dinner is usually something Lia will order with the money I leave her." My mom answers for us all.

She is sitting up straight in the orange plastic chair as if she is on the witness stand in the courtroom. I want to question this witness but refrain from doing so to save us some time. I quickly shove the apple under the blanket. It's obviously not doing what I intended for it to do.

Dr. Cramer inches closer to me and looks me in the eye. I can see some gray eyebrow hairs on his bushy eyebrows above his bifo-cals. There are about three on the left and five on his right.

"Is there anything you'd like to add, Lia?" he asks with a whiff of wintergreen entering the room.

I bet you he has a bottle of spray mouth freshener in his white coat that he uses throughout the day.

"No," I respond as politely as possible to ensure complete compliance with this authority.

He goes on to ask a long list of questions that have to do with how I am doing at school, at home, with peers, etc. It is a mix of investigation and the 20 Questions game we play on long car rides. He asks my parents to leave about half an hour later. They walk together out the door, and my dad closes the door behind them. Thanks, Dad, for always respecting my privacy.

As I sit in the room with Dr. Cramer looking at me, I begin to wonder if this will result in a one-to-one versus a one-on-one. I'm hoping it's one-to-one.

"Lia, can you tell me about this new relationship your mother mentioned?" he asks.

"Sure. It's not too new. I've known him since the beginning of the summer, and he has been with me a lot since then. Things are good." I politely correct him from my mom's misinformation.

"What kinds of things do you two do together?"

"We run together. He pushes me to be better. More disciplined. I share a lot with him, and I feel like he helps me get better grades, have more structure, and just do better."

"Can you give me some examples?" he requests.

"I study longer than ever. I am now getting straight As. I eat healthier like my mom has been trying to get me to do for years, and I run harder, which got our school the win at Nationals last week."

"And what happens if you don't do those things?" he asks curiously.

"That's only happened a few times, and it's usually okay. He just helps me do more the next time to make up for lacking."

"Do you feel safe in this relationship?" he blatantly asks.

"I do. He's kind of like my security blanket if I was five." I snicker, trying to bring humor into this serious conversation.

"Was he there when you fainted?" he asks, scribbling notes on his yellow legal pad.

"No. But I was thinking of him when I awoke. Most of my day is spent that way." I smile.

"Okay, Lia. I'm going to discuss things with your parents. The nurse has ordered you a tray from the cafeteria. I'd like for you to see what you can do with eating something. Okay?"

I'm guessing this is a rhetorical question since his back is already on the other side of the door, and he is speaking to the nurse.

Great. More attempts at making me ingest something. Can't I just be left alone and go home now? Ed, did you hear that? Can you come eat with me? I really don't want to be here alone.

Quick, use math. How many calories are in the apple hiding beneath the blanket? Now, add that to the black coffee. Good. Now add in the piece of Juicy Fruit gum. Okay. Now, subtract the mileage I ran this morning. And that equals?

"Lia, I've brought you a tray." Nurse Joyce interrupts my math equation and adds more to the problem.

Okay, one individual-sized carton of chocolate milk. Now add three bites of the turkey sandwich. Just three. Enough to show effort but not enough to do me harm. And one handful of cooked broccoli. Things just got challenging! What a curveball! I have no idea if the broccoli was steamed, brushed with olive oil, or topped with butter. My palate isn't distinguished enough to discern between them. Now, I'm stumped. Perhaps I shall forgo the broccoli. Okay, next is the chocolate chip cookie wrapped in saran wrap. Does the saran wrap suffocate the caloric intake in any way? Not sure. That is more of a science question. I want to stick with math.

"How's the food?" My mom and dad walk in before my equation is complete. Darn, I hate it when that happens.

"I'm not hungry," I lie. I do feel a growling sensation at the pit of my stomach, but I'd rather wait to eat at home, where I have access to packaged items, which helps my math equations move along quickly and more precisely than this one. I feel better when I know as opposed to when I don't know. Ed always lets me know what is working and what is not with us. I rarely feel like I need to guess or estimate things. I like this. He is easy to understand, although others have described him as being very difficult to understand. But I can tell when I have impressed him or disappointed him. He is very direct with me. He doesn't leave me reading between the lines.

"Honey, you need to eat, or else the doctors will not let you leave," my dad states sternly.

"Isn't force-feeding a violation of my human rights?" I sarcastically respond as I bite into the turkey sandwich. One bite, two left, according to today's daily math equation. Ed is a math whiz and would be impressed if I get it right today.

"Mr. and Mrs. Lloyd, may I speak with you in the hallway for a minute?" requests Dr. Cramer, the balder one.

My intestines tighten, my throat swells, and my heart races. I really hope I don't choke on my next bite.

"Can't you just say what you need to say here?" I request politely. After all, I'm eating like they wanted me to. The least they can do is let me in on the conversation that will be about me.

Dr. Cramer looks at me and then at my parents, waiting for their response. The problem is, if you knew my parents, you would know by now that they provide very little parental direction. Good luck getting the response you are looking for.

"We need to admit Lia upstairs for further observation," Dr. Cramer announces.

"Okay," both my parents say in unison.

What? How can they just throw me to the lions like this? And why are they now in agreement with each other?

Chapter 7

"Lia, time to wake up!" says Nurse Wanda from my room 233 doorway.

In my moment between dreaming and waking, I mistake Nurse Wanda for my mom. I despise my brother or her waking me up only to have me wait on them in the driveway. But I would take that over being here. I open my eyes and see Nurse Wanda, a short woman with gray hair and goggles for eyeglasses. She smiles so wide it's hard not to smile back. She holds on tight to her clipboard, makes a checkmark next to my name, and moves down to 235 next door.

I'm scared. I have no idea who anyone is, what to do, or where to go. My bathroom is locked, and there are no clothes for me to change into for the day. My normal routine of grooming and dressing is not an option. I wish I were home.

I peek my head out into the hallway. I am dressed in a pale blue hospital gown, different from the zoo animal one from downstairs. I also have a new set of plastic ID bracelets. I see others dressed like me standing in a line at the nurses' station. Who are they, and am I supposed to be there, too?

I really wish I had my beloved hoodie. It is cold here. Sadly, last night, I learned that any clothing from the outside is contraband. Another patient in the room next to mine mentioned that when we make it to the next level in our treatment plan, we are escorted downstairs (a step closer to the front doors that release you from this hell), and it is there that I can have my hoodie. I didn't catch her name.

I shuffle down the corridor and join the others in line at the nurses' station. I look at the faces of those in line, but I don't see the girl next door to me. Some of the girls are talking to each other, and two of the boys are trying to expose each other through the hospital gown openings. Thankfully, Nurse Wanda quickly puts a stop to this.

Last night, Dr. Cramer walked my mom, dad, and me through the schedule of this second floor during the admission process, but I was in complete shock from it all. The fact that I had to stay at the hospital and was not allowed to go home threw me into a whirlwind. Luckily, I was able to reach out to Ed and was busy speaking with him throughout the whole process. I almost missed my parents hugging me goodnight before they turned and walked out the double-locked doors. I didn't say anything in return to them. I only responded to Ed. I am furious that they have left me here. Nobody can answer me when I ask them how long I must stay here or why

I am even here. The only reply I get is, "Lia, you need help that home cannot offer you right now."

"Lia, here are your meds. Please take them, then line up to get weight and vitals," another nurse named Nancy says as I place my hands out. She must have read the confused look on my face because she quickly reassures me by saying, "Don't worry, I know you have not had your assessment yet with Dr. Cramer. This is just a daily multivitamin."

"Okay," I mumble as I gulp the huge pill. Whatever happened to chewable vitamins that don't try to tear down your uvula? I shuffle over to the second line of blue gowns waiting their turn. To occupy my time, I observe as Nurse Nancy continues to dispense medications. I can't help but notice her red cowboy boots and eccentric style. She's got long, thick hair and appears to be in her late thirties. I miss having thick hair like that. It seems mine has been falling out in the shower faster than I can grow it.

"Next," she states.

I look back to the line and watch as another girl climbs onto a numberless metal square and then sits in the chair to get her arm squeezed by a cuff and get her temperature taken. In one way, I am impressed with the order and timing of all these people working together at once. In another way, I am saddened by the flocking of us sheep-like patients being herded by the staff.

"I'm not getting on. You can't make me," shouts a girl with blonde hair and blue eyes. I watch as she stomps her pink-painted toenails, noticing she is also revolting against wearing the required blue sock slippers.

"Zoey, you need to step on," Nurse Wanda compassionately replies.

"No. I won't," argues Zoey.

"I know it is difficult, but I promise you will be okay," reassures Nurse Wanda. That woman has the patience of a monk.

"No—if the number goes up, then I get my pass home for the weekend. If it doesn't, then I am locked here even longer," cries Zoey.

"Yes, that is right, Zoey. You need to step on," calmly states Nurse Wanda.

"Fine!" Zoey stomps onto the numberless scale. She stands there for a few seconds, staring at the blank white wall ahead of her. When she steps off, she begs to be given an answer on whether she has gained weight, but Nurse Wanda calmly reminds her that her treatment team can discuss this with her tomorrow.

"You will be able to attend the treatment team tomorrow afternoon. We do it every Tuesday," Thalia shares with me.

"Cool, thanks," I say shyly back.

"Basically, everyone sits around this big round table like we're getting ready to play a game of poker. Patient versus staff members. But instead, they discuss your prescribed treatment plan with you," Thalia sarcastically states.

"Hopefully, we are all on the same page about me leaving this place by the weekend," I say optimistically.

"Don't count on it." Thalia mumbles, and just like that my hope deflates.

"Time to get to group therapy. Everyone, follow me," Nurse Nancy says. We all follow her red cowboy boots and long swinging ponytail down the hall to the group room.

The next twelve hours are one long string of pee, eat, therapy group, pee, eat, therapy group, etc. After our last group of the evening, I'm exhausted. My mind is numb, but my body is shaking with restlessness. I need to find a way out of here.

"Everyone, line up for your bedtime medications," Nurse Wanda instructs. Another line forms at the nurses' station.

"There you go. You've got me!" I snark at the night Nurse Wanda, who is claiming that I am "cheeking" my medicines. I am learning that this place has its own language. "Cheeking" is when a patient hoards their pills like a squirrel in their cheeks to refrain from ingesting the intoxicating prescriptions that Dr. Cramer had chosen for them. Being it is my second night here, but my first one taking nighttime meds, I attempted to "cheek" but failed. I'll need more practice. It seems to be a delicate blend of swallowing without ingesting and quickly walking away to spit them out before dissolving in my saliva. But not too fast because I don't want to raise the suspicion of the nurses.

This time, I was caught. Now I know that Nurse Wanda is good! I should have guessed because she's been here the longest. I think she suffers from paranoia, and that is what makes her good at checking for "cheeking." I like paranoid people; they amuse me. They are thorough and determined, leaving no stone unturned. Nurse Wanda reminds me of my Ed in this way. Ed usually assumes that he knows what is best for me. And recently, he has been right. He has me questioning my beliefs, and I am really opening my mind up. I have noticed that we are thinking a lot alike now. Like a set of siamese twins - we are spending so much time together our thoughts and actions are becoming more alike.

Which is weird, right? I remember watching a 60-minute episode on a pair of Siamese twins and how they were thinking about getting surgery to separate, but the risks were too high. What a tough predicament to be in. I don't know what I would do in that situation. I guess it would depend on how well I got along with my connected twin. But I really am more of an introvert and prefer my time alone to replenish, which is why this place is draining me. And not only emotionally draining me through the meals and group therapy sessions today but literally draining tubes of blood from me. Are they donating pints of my type A blood to earn some extra cash? Or are they cloning me in a warehouse? Whichever it is, one of me is enough. We don't need multiple Lia Lloyds occupying space and utilizing precious oxygen on this global-warming-wracked planet. But I should at least get a percentage of the sales if they are cashing in on my blood.

I shuffle from the nurses' station to my room, 233, for the night. The tile floors are cold and white. They're clean because they were mopped this morning and evening by the custodian, Carl. Carl is an amazing singer. He doesn't know that I heard him sing under his breath as he shined the floors this evening, but I did. I have no idea why he isn't pursuing his vocal talent further than the halls of this hospital. But maybe he is, and I just don't know. He waxes the floors so well that I can see my reflection as I shuffle to my room.

The hospital provides us with slipper socks during our stay at this level. A slipper sock is an extended relative of the spork that we use at mealtimes. We are not allowed knives or forks due to the harm we could use them for. They also tend to serve mostly casserole-type foods that are spork-friendly. A slipper sock is just what it sounds like it would be: a sock with a slip-proof bottom of a slipper. I suppose by making these mandatory, the hospital protects itself from any liability of possible falls. Same with the spork, the hospital is protecting itself from the patients hurting themselves or one another, which also protects the hospital from getting hurt financially.

After a few minutes of tossing and turning, trying to get comfortable, I lay my head down on my vinyl-covered pillow and mattress. They are cold, and a brief case of goosebumps overtakes my body. It's like I'm sleeping in an igloo. I scrunch up in the fetal position to create as much body heat as I can. I pretend I am cuddling with Ed. I close my eyes and begin to visualize the beach; I am harnessing the power of the sun to warm up. Visualization is a skill they push onto us here. Maybe they can invest in smart heating or allow us to wear layers of clothing. But instead, they provide us with the skill of visualization. I suppose it cuts down on the utility costs for the building.

Chapter 8

"Good morning, Lia. How are you feeling today?" asks Dr. Cramer from across the room, sitting in his brown leather swivel office chair. He is dressed in business khakis and a buttoned-down, pin-striped shirt. He resembles a candy cane from a certain angle. His boat shoes are worn at the big toe, making me wonder if his feet are still growing in his fifties. His gray, bushy eyebrows overgrow his eyeglass frames. He looks me in the eye when speaking to me. I immediately feel uncomfortable. Eye contact makes me crawl out of my skin—especially with someone in authority.

"I don't know." I give him an honest reply and stare at his forehead to avoid the discomfort I am feeling. I begin to scan the neatly lined, framed diplomas hanging on the wall behind his big, brown leather chair. They are precisely aligned. I imagine that a ruler was involved in these hangings. I focus on the parallel frames and appreciate their symmetry. It is calming to look at.

"Okay. Let's start by looking at the feeling wheel, and you can choose one or two of them that feel relevant to you." He pulls out a laminated worksheet that looks a lot like the wheel in the Wheel of Fortune episodes that my grandpa watches while my grandma cleans up the dinner table. But this wheel has words I am supposed to choose from. I reach out and grab the wheel and quickly realize why it is laminated. I imagine the temptation to crumple, tear, or wad it up is high for many of us here. The lamination protects this sheet and acts as its shield. I respect that.

"Okay. I guess I feel sad and mad," I reply, dragging my finger across the wheel to connect the two.

"That's a great start, Lia. What do you think is causing you to feel these things?" Dr. Cramer asks curiously.

"I'm mad that I am here. And I am sad that Ed is not here, too."

"Okay. I understand," he confidently replies.

"But can you? I mean, you get to wear your own clothes and leave this place each day while I can't," I argue.

"That's a good point, Lia. However, I can empathize with you without having to be experiencing the same thing that you are."

"I don't believe that is true."

"Okay. Well, let's start with you missing Ed. Is this the first time you've taken time away from Ed?"

"Yes, but it isn't my choice. You guys won't let him be here."

"And why do you think this is?"

"Because you all think you know what is best for me and force that down my throat instead of letting me choose for myself. I am being treated like a child here."

"That makes sense that you feel the rules and structure here are confining. Do you have rules and structure at home?"

"No. We did have some when my dad lived with us, but since he moved out, it's different."

"How so?"

"My mom says we're grounded but then lets us do whatever we want. It makes no sense when she says one thing and does another. It is confusing. My brother loves this about her, but it irritates me." I sigh. I'm exhausted. How much talking will I have to do each day I am here?

"Do you like to know what is expected of you, Lia?" Dr. Cramer leans forward in his seat and eagerly waits for my answer.

"Yes. It makes sense to want to know how things should be instead of being surprised when I try and don't hit the mark because I didn't know." I am beginning to get annoyed. Doesn't he know the obvious answer here?

"Does Ed let you know what is expected of you, Lia?"

"Yes. And he lets me know if I did well or not. And if I don't, he lets me know how to do better."

"I see. Doesn't the staff here do the same?" Dr. Cramer asks, his forehead wrinkling.

"Yes, but I don't know them the same way that I know Ed. I trust him. I don't trust you guys," I reply as I look back at the neatly-lined, framed diplomas.

"Well, I hope you can begin to do so while you are here," he replies, sitting back in his chair.

"I don't plan to be here long enough. When can I go home?" I am desperately seeking an answer that I will like.

"Lia, there is a lot going on in your life right now, and I want to help you learn healthy ways to respond to it all. Once we work through things, we will get you back home. How does that sound?"

"It sounds vague and like you are avoiding the question. How long do I have to be here?"

"It greatly depends on several things, Lia…" he pauses before finishing.

"Again, thanks for your clarity and preciseness. If only you could be as precise with answering me as you were when hanging your fancy degrees from your overpriced universities," I interrupt his thoughts.

I get up and stomp out of the room. I make sure to slam the door behind me. My intent is to shake and rattle his perfectly aligned diplomas. I want them to feel the way I feel right now: unhinged.

Chapter 9

"Good evening. In tonight's group, we are going to practice a coping skill called guided visualization. Please grab a yoga mat and lay down on your back with your eyes closed," Nurse Wanda announces as she unrolls her flamingo-pink mat.

I do as I am told, which is the best strategy here. I grab a sky-blue mat and unroll it. I lay down on my back. The floor is hard, and my spine aches. I slowly close my eyes.

"With your eyes closed, please take a moment and think of your safe place," Nurse Wanda speaks softly, slightly louder than a whisper.

I begin to imagine the warm, white sand on the beach with the sun shining so bright I must close my eyes. I smell the coconut of the thick suntan lotion. And I hear the sound of the ocean waves crashing on the shore. I inhale and exhale as Nurse Wanda instructs.

"Continue to inhale, 1, 2, 3… and exhale, 1, 2, 3. Imagine what you see, hear, smell, taste, and touch in your safe place. Try to engage all your senses. Know that you can come to this safe place at any time you need to." Nurse Wanda slows her speaking.

"You gotta be kidding me?!" I gasp and sit up straight as can be on my mat. I must have startled the others because Nurse Wanda is shushing everyone and encouraging them to lie back down.

"Lia, what is happening for you?" she checks in with me between shushes.

"I'm sorry. I just can't do this," I mumble as I lay back down on my mat to try and decrease the number of eyes staring at me.

"Sure you can. Start again by inhaling 1, 2, 3. And exhale 1, 2, 3. Everyone join us, please."

But I can't! While I was enjoying my sunbathing, a tsunami struck. Everything in its path is washed away. I am no longer safe here. I quickly think of being high on a mountaintop, safe from possible flooding. I am at the peak, seeing breathtaking views from all around. I breathe in the fresh, crisp air. I smell fresh pine, like the little pine tree car air freshener hanging from my rearview mirror in my student driver's education vehicle. I feel safe. Until a snow avalanche rushes down with tremendous velocity and takes me and the trees with it. I am no longer safe here. I go higher to the skies in a helicopter, which crashes to pieces within minutes of flying. I am not safe here, either.

"When you are ready, it is time to leave your safe place and come back to the present," Nurse Wanda invites us back to our sad reality.

I sit up and open my eyes wide, ready to embrace the present, even if it means being locked up here in the hospital. At least there are no known natural disasters waiting for me.

"Are you okay, Lia?" asks Nurse Wanda.

I suppose my jack-in-the-box spring-up drew attention to me once again. "Yeah, I'm okay."

"Okay. I want to remind everyone to open your eyes and sit up very slowly."

They do that here. They speak to us individually while simultaneously announcing it to the whole room. I suppose it keeps us from feeling singled out, but you do feel that way when you know they are talking about you.

"Does anyone want to share about their safe place?" Nurse Wanda inquires of the group.

"I will," eagerly offers Zoey. You get participation points for sharing in group therapy. Each point gets you closer to downstairs. Zoey must really want to get there because she has been voluntarily exposing herself to the group all week.

"My safe place is the cabin at the lake my family goes to each summer. We've been going since I was a baby," discloses Zoey.

"Thank you for sharing, Zoey. What about the cabin at the lake brings you feelings of safety and security?" Nurse Wanda takes notes on her notepad so she can add this information to the private charts that only staff and parents have access to. They are about us, so it would only make sense for us to be able to read them, too.

"I just have good memories of me being there with my parents and brothers. We stay up late around the fire my brothers build. We eat s'mores and play board games. I am the champion at Monopoly," Zoey continues to slowly reveal herself to us.

"That does sound like a safe place. And during recreational hours, remind us to get a game of Monopoly started!" declares Nurse Wanda.

Sure, it does sound safe until someone trips and falls into the fire. Or they forget to put it out, and it spreads across the land. Is there anywhere that is safe enough to be called a "safe place?"

"Would anyone else like to share?" Nurse Wanda asks as she looks around the room. I am learning that the trick to not getting called on to share is to avoid making eye contact with the group facilitator while also showing them that you are paying attention and present. It is being neutral.

"Okay, well, if no one else wants to share, we will leave the last couple minutes of the group to roll up our mats, put them away, and wash our hands before snack time." Nurse Wanda sounds much too excited for snack time.

I roll my mat up like I used to roll sushi with my dad in our granite counter kitchen. The sushi we made was not made with fish because we had a tank of fish in our home, and things could have gotten weird between them and me. I had worked well with our fish: Mathew, Mark, Luke, and John. I had trained them to swim up to the surface when I turned the fish tank light on. Mathew, Mark, Luke, and John all swim to the surface and eagerly wait. It is then that I reward them with their flakes of fish food and watch them swim in circles, excited for the feast. If only I could get that excited for today's snack time. I walk with my rolled-up mat and place it back with the others in the corner of the room. Some are rolled tighter than others, and this feels like an itch that I cannot scratch. I feel this itch often. It's not an allergy, a bite, or a rash. It just sits somewhere in my body that irks me until all things are equal. In this instance, all yoga mats rolled in the same tightness. Ed gets this. He helps me make things more equal, more even, fairer. Other people in my life have suggested that I be more flexible and accept the insistent itching. But they have not themselves experienced this insatiable itch. The kind that feels worse than your sock seams being unaligned in your sneakers that are double-knotted and impossible to untie to realign.

"Everyone follow me," Nurse Wanda instructs the group of us teenagers, who can easily be mistaken for a flock of sheep because we all migrate towards her and walk down the hall to the dining room, where we spend much of our time.

"Remember, crew, no napkins." I find this confusing since the sporks are packaged with napkins, and it feels like a disastrous environmental waste for us to throw away clean napkins. Nurse Wanda explained to me that some people like to wrap their food in napkins and save it for later, which breaks the rule of NO FOOD ALLOWED OUTSIDE THE DINING ROOM. Another option for napkin use is for others to hide it to dispose of before leaving the dining room, which breaks the rule of MUST COMPLETE ALL MEALS AND SNACKS. This place is big on promoting no food waste. Yet, paper waste is enforced.

As instructed, I dispose of my unused napkin. It hurts to admit to this, as it is going against every value I hold. But I suppose it is getting easier to do each time I'm asked. I chalk it up to my learning to compromise some. I've been told I'm a bit stubborn. Ed has been teaching me to do the same. There were things he would request that we do, and at first, I would feel bad doing them, but over time, they've gotten easier, and now I understand why they are a must. And it feels good to understand Ed in this way, and feel like we are a team.

"Okay, snack time starts now. You have fifteen minutes to complete," announces Nurse Wanda as she picks up her white spork.

You would think that we are at Nathan's famous hot-dog-eating championship being aired on ESPN each year, but we are not. We are sitting in the cold dining room on the second floor of this children's hospital in New York, dressed in our matching blue hospital gowns and sock slippers, simultaneously holding our sporks in our dominant hands, getting ready to shovel the yogurt into our mouths. Along with another item, of course, because snack time requires us to choose two items from the cart.

"Does anyone want to play a game? We have several to choose from," Nurse Wanda excitedly asks. I bet she was a cheerleader in her high school years or maybe the school mascot. I feel like Chloe and her would get along great. I do miss Chloe, even though she made me super mad by betraying me and Ed.

"I do!" pipes in Zoey, as though she has just given her marriage vows to Justin Bieber, of whom she has numerous posters hung in her bedroom at home waiting to be stared at for hours again after her discharge. Something has come over Zoey. She seems a bit different. Maybe happier?

"Great. If anyone else wants to jump in, do so."

The two of them, eventually joined by Thalia, complete a round of Would You Rather? Cards. Brandon, a new patient, also jumps in. I bet he did so for the participation points. I did the same on my first few days, hoping those points would get me downstairs faster. They tell us this when we are admitted. But what they don't tell you is more involved than that. He will figure this out soon enough. For sure, at his first roundtable experience.

The yogurt is advertised as smooth and creamy on its label, but I find it hard to swallow. I have lumps in my throat, which could possibly be an enlarged lymph node, throat cancer, or worry. I would mention this to Nurse Wanda, but table topics are supposed to be light and fun. My undiagnosed throat lump may not fit that description. If I do end up choking due to restricted airways, I am in a hospital with essential staff and equipment, which reassures me of my chances of survival.

"We've got five minutes left. Let's finish up."

The pressure is on. Five minutes to complete. I have never been one to perform well under time constraints. I am concerned about my performance on the upcoming standardized tests in high school. Five minutes. I can do that. That is four laps around the track for me, which can equate to ten spoonfuls of my Dannon yogurt. Ed reminds me often that I am not a quitter. So, I swallow and disregard the lump that is trying to derail my progress here. I focus on the spoon-like scoop of the spork and disregard the four fork-like tines. Is it more of a fork or more of a spoon or equally both? I don't know.

"Okay, time is up. Please move away from the table. Brandon and Thalia, you need to stay behind to supplement. The others can follow Nurse Mary to the recreational room. Zoey, can you get Monopoly set up?" The herd of us do as we are told.

I help Zoey set up the Monopoly board. Throughout setting up, she willingly shares with me her strategy of building on Park Place and Boardwalk. I stay quiet about my strategy for today's game, which is to try and secure the orange places. Over the last few games I've played here, I've realized that the orange places are the ones to snatch and build on. Based on the science of probability, my orange spaces get landed on more by the other players due to their proximity to the "in jail" space. I've learned to let Zoey dream big for her dark blue spaces.

"Can I be the Top Hat? I am always the Top Hat."

I hope Zoe chooses another piece.

Chapter 10

Today is Treatment Team Tuesday. It's a big day on this floor. It's what Thalia refers to as "Tense Tuesday" because her anxiety is highest these days, and why Zoey was panicking at vitals and weights yesterday. That data determined the team's next moves for her.

"Lia, it's your turn," Nurse Wanda winks at me as she invites me to follow her into room 221, the conference room. I take a seat in the only empty folding chair at the large round table. Process of elimination tells me this is where I should be. Dr. Cramer, Nurse Nancy, Nurse Wanda, and two new doctors in white coats are sitting around the table. Dr. Cramer begins to explain what Thalia had already informed me of: the importance of the treatment plan.

"Lia, welcome to the treatment team. We will be meeting as a team each week. Before we get started, we'd like to get your permission for our resident, Cat, to sit in for learning purposes only.

What do you think?" Dr. Cramer asks me in front of all the others as if I actually have a choice in this decision.

I look over at Cat, a blonde-haired, blue-eyed woman dressed in a white coat who introduces herself as a resident. She smiles at me. I instantly feel like a lab rat and want to refuse, but instead, I swallow my thoughts and feelings of rage.

"It's fine," I say as I smile and nod yes to get out of the spotlight as soon as possible.

"And I am Dr. J, It's abbreviated." introduces the other new doctor sitting at the table in a white coat. He has a notepad and pen with him, either for doodling or taking notes on this awkward encounter.

Is Dr. J an informant for the FBI? A ghostwriter for a well-known publication? Why would he have an abbreviated name? I suppose the answer lies somewhere in the fine print of a document somewhere in the pile of papers my parents signed upon my arrival.

"I oversee the staff on this unit and the one downstairs," he informs me as though he can read my mind.

I need to remember this guy; he is the ultimate boss, and if Dr. Cramer screws up, I know who to tell.

"Lia, what are your goals while being here?" asks Nurse Nancy. She's the one with the crazy red cowboy boots. I am really starting to like her. She's someone you can tell is happy and free with being themselves regardless of what others may think. She's brave.

"I don't know. To leave before the weekend?" I ask.

I am shocked at the laughing response of the panel members. I was not trying to be humorous.

"We need you to complete your treatment plan first, Lia. And that won't happen in a week," Dr. J explains.

"Okay, well, what's on this thing?" I ask in my most annoyed tone. I really want to let them know that I am not a stand-up comedian for their entertainment.

"First, we must identify what your needs are and how we can teach you skills to meet them. A large part of treatment is using cognitive behavioral therapy to learn new skills and help you develop healthier relationships…" Dr. J goes on to list the treatment goals, but all I can think about is my relationship with Ed. The others at the table are nodding their heads in agreement.

"Do you have any questions about this plan?" Dr. Cramer asks me. Again, in front of the whole room.

"I don't think so," I say as I sink into the metal folding chair.

"Okay, well, let us know if you do. We will meet again next week."

I walk out of room 221. I have no real idea of what just happened. But I will admit that they are good. They almost had me believing the treatment plan is something we created as a team, but I know the truth: it is them vs. me. I guess I will just have to play along to get what I need, which is my freedom or, at the very least, my hoodie. That would be nice.

"Lia, it's time for the group. What did they say to you?" asks Thalia. I am thankful for her warning of what Treatment Team Tuesdays here look like before I entered that lion's den.

"Okay. Not much. You?" I force these words out because I am still unsure as to what just happened at that roundtable.

"I got a pass for the weekend! Finally!" she shrieks with excitement.

"Yay!" I do my best to fake excitement for her. Inside, I feel fierce jealousy at the thought of her being able to walk out of those locked double doors and experience life.

"It only took six weeks of being here!" she says in a serious tone. I try to identify any hint of sarcasm in her statement, but I don't sense any. I think she is being serious.

"Seriously?!" I say hastily, using my whole body to get the words out.

"Yeah. And apparently, the team says that is quick." She shrugs her shoulders and pulls me into the group therapy room.

I slump down into a tan metal folding chair that feels hard and cold, and I am miserable. They have ten of them all facing each other in a circle as if we are all gathering around a campfire, getting ready to make s'mores and sing Kumbaya. But instead, we will be going around sharing our names and stating what we are feeling at this moment.

"Hi, I'm Lia, and I am feeling fine."

"Lia, remember what it means when you say fine. It's not a real feeling," reminds eccentric Nurse Nancy, sitting with her legs crossed, swinging her red cowboy boot. I want to tell her to stop swinging it because it is far too distracting, but I move forward with changing my feeling and check in, instead.

"I'm Lia, and I am feeling hopeful."

"Thank you, Lia. Next is Thalia," Nurse Nancy buys into my act and allows the group's attention to move to my right. I feel relieved when all eyes shift to Thalia. I cannot stand feeling eyes on me; it makes my skin crawl. Ed says it's because I'm not confident enough, and I worry that others are judging my body and appearance. There might be some truth to that. But I also think it is because I don't want people to find out how weird I really am inside. He thinks I can get more confident by changing my appearance and body. So, we have been lifting weights after track practice, and I've been growing my hair out. Apparently, long hair and being "strong" is what's considered beautiful right now. I personally don't understand why I need to do all this hard work to be "in" for now when, over time, it'll be a different look, and I'll have to change again. I despise change. But I have been told that I don't always know what's best, which is why I rely on Ed.

"Good. Now that everyone has checked in let's get to today's group topic: family and relationships. I'm going to ask all of you to think of someone in your life who you feel safe around," guides Nurse Nancy.

My dad. Always my dad.

"Now, does this person also provide boundaries, clear expectations, and structure to your life?" continues Nurse Nancy, who is now our emotional and mental tour guide.

He used to. Not so much anymore. The last time I saw him was downstairs almost a week ago. Before that, it had been two months. He hasn't been the same since he moved out. I guess he doesn't make the cut for this visualization. But Ed does. Way to go, Ed, for saving the day. This wouldn't be your first time.

"When you are ready, let's go around the room and share who came to mind for you," explains Nurse Nancy, thankfully no longer swinging that red boot of hers as she speaks.

"My mom. She's always there when I need her. It's been so hard being away from her while here," Thalia shares.

"That's great, Thalia. I am sure she misses you, too, and is excited to see you this weekend for a pass," replies Nurse Nancy.

Ouch, salt in the wound. Wish I had a pass this weekend. Zoey must feel the same because she blurts out, "It's not fair. I have done everything they asked and still don't get a pass," and storms out of the room. She sure is a firecracker.

"Okay. Can I have everyone take a deep breath, please? I know that Tuesdays are tricky with the treatment team happening, but let's try to be present in the group. Who is ready to go next?" Nurse Nancy calmly speaks.

"I'll go. I thought of my dad but then changed it to Ed." I choose to share this with the group because I figure it's best to get it over with. I did the same when I was five years old and was being forced to eat a pile of lima beans. I ate them first to get them off my plate and out of sight, then moved on to the delicious mashed potatoes and meatloaf. This tactic slays anticipatory anxieties.

"Lia, can you share more about Ed?" she insists.

"Sure. He's kind of been my everything lately. We have gotten super close."

"That's great that you have support, Lia. Who wants to go next?"

That was close. I really did not want to betray Ed by speaking about him to a group of strangers who may not understand what we have. Thank you, Nurse Nancy, for moving on to the others. I promise not to allow the swinging of your red cowboy boot to bother me so much if you choose to swing it again. Ed, did you hear how important you are to me? I hope you know that.

The rest of the group finishes sharing. Before we are allowed to leave the room, we must set an intention for our snack session coming up next. This always trips me up.

"My intention is to eat mindfully," I lie through a grin. Who am I kidding? I plan to think of Ed the whole time. It's the only thing that forces me to not lose my appetite and swallow every bite of the Nutri-Grain bars they insist I finish.

Chapter 11

"Good morning. Happy Tuesday! It's going to be a terrific day!" announces Nurse Wanda from my doorway. This is how she likes to wake me before the sunrise. At first, I found it more annoying than at home when Cole or my mom would wake me at my doorway. Now, I find it endearing, especially because her wide smile wins me over every time. She is like a grandma who comes to visit around the holidays and tries to make up for her 11-month absence by showering you with love and gifts. However, due to this hospital's program policies, patients are not allowed to accept gifts of any kind from the staff, and vice versa. Yet, I am certain that if gift-giving were allowed, Nurse Wanda would deliver neatly wrapped presents, a handmade card, and a decorative bow that you'd want to save.

Today is Tuesday, which means they are serving tacos for lunch in the cafeteria. There are team-building activities for recreational hours, and I am invited to attend the good ol' treatment team meeting. This hospital runs on themes. As much as I hate to admit it, the predictability of these themes is starting to grow on me. Each day, I know what to expect, which is so different from my life outside of here. People are here every hour of the day and night, which felt invasive at first, but I now find it comforting.

Before I met Ed, I spent a lot of time alone after my dad moved out. My mom was worried that I was isolating and depressed, but I must continuously remind her that I am not. I am just not as social as her and my brother. I am different from them. I am okay with being alone. I do like Ed being with me. He has a way of being present without being completely noticeable in the limelight.

Soon, I'll be making my way to the roundtable room 221 when I'm called. I hope they call for me during breakfast hour. Oatmeal is on the menu today, and I wouldn't be upset about skipping its lumpiness. Either be lumpy or be cream of wheat. Pick a side. Same with crunchy peanut butter. Can't stand it. Be creamy and completely blended, or stay a peanut. Why try to be both?

"Lia, when you are done getting your meds, vitals, and weight, come to the dining room, please," Nurse Nancy shares as she waltzes down the hall in her red cowboy boots. Classic. The red cowboy boots and the fact that I won't be missing breakfast today after all. I'll have to face off with the lumps. If I don't engage with them, then I'm strongly encouraged to drink a shake of some sort that my dad had to drink for weeks when his jaw was wired shut. It is overly sweet and smells like medicine. But it may have to be today's breakfast, depending on the size of the lumps.

For now, I must try to play the part of a compliant and eager-to-get-well patient. I have felt numb since I arrived exactly thirteen days, three hours, and forty-six minutes ago. I know that it will be difficult to pep myself up enough to convince the roundtable how excited I am to be living my life. I played Snoopy at summer camp when I was ten, which surprised my family due to my reserved nature. I think it was the cute dog costume that made me consider this part; I can't remember. But I know my acting skills must be somewhat average if I got the part. Let me see if I can connect with my inner Snoopy during this meeting.

"Lia, you know that you must finish your meal. How can I support you?" Nurse Nancy places her calloused hands on mine. I have been meaning to ask her what her hobbies are. Ax throwing? Rope climbing? Woodworking? I know she does something with her hands.

"I know. I just can't swallow these lumps," I say, looking down at my bowl of oatmeal, which is not willing to pick a side in the world of textures.

"Okay, then what flavor Ensure do you want? Vanilla or chocolate?" she asks.

I don't want either of them, but I comply. "Chocolate," I choke out. At least I can pretend it's the chocolate frosty my dad and I would get at the hamburger place on Fridays after ballet class.

Why can't they just make this thick brown cup of fluid intravenous to skip the taste buds and gag reflex?

"Here you are. You have ten minutes to complete it," Nurse Nancy sets the filled cup down.

I stare at it, wishing I had telekinetic powers to bring it to the sink without the staff noticing. Or to poke a hole at the bottom of the cup, drill a hole into the table, and have a stream of it slowly drain from the cup.

"You okay, Lia?" she asks me.

"Yeah," I reply, frustrated that my ideas to get rid of this supplement are not ones that I can possibly get down to in ten minutes, probably nine by now. I pick up the cup, throw my head back, stare at the white tiled ceiling, wondering where the air vents lead, chug the supplement down with minimal use of my taste buds, and swallow a few times. I sit back up and immediately feel sick to my stomach. I want to go home.

"Good job," claps Nurse Nancy.

I follow her into the group therapy room for the first group of the day on this terrible Tuesday. I choose the same chair that I have had since day one. We don't have assigned seats, but I like sitting here. I don't know what I would do if someone else tried to sit here. I look around the room and don't see Zoey or Thalia. They must be getting ready for their rounds at the treatment team or plotting how to escape from this place.

Group starts with all of us going around and stating our names as usual and then having to share what color we most feel like today. I don't feel like a box of Crayola crayons—I just don't. And I wonder how someone with color vision deficiency does with this check-in question. Why can't we just state what we are feeling instead?

Today's group is based on team building with our peers. I am supposed to be open to the idea of falling backward off a chair into the arms of three of my peers. I am not open to this. It sounds impulsive and unsafe. If Ed were here, I might consider it because he always catches me when I fall. But I barely know these people and have been taught by my mom from a very early age not to trust strangers. She gave me a whole lesson on stranger danger each year, adding more information as I aged.

"Lia, remember you need to participate if you want points for attending a group today," reminds Heath, a new staff member who looks like a college frat boy. The hospital calls the blue-scrubbed staff members "techs." I was very confused at first, thinking they were referring to technology, but they are not robots; they are re-al-life humans.

"I know. I know," I respond between gritted teeth.

I don't think I will be able to do this one. I don't want to die, despite what the doctors here may assume. Besides, where are Zoey and Thalia? Why aren't they being given a chance to risk their lives like this?

"Heath, where are Zoey and Thalia?" I ask.

"They moved to level two," he says, pointing to the floor.

You must be kidding me. Those lucky ladies have traded in their blue hospital gowns for their flannel pajama pants and hood-ies on the first floor, one step closer to the exits. I want to join them in Hoodie Heaven.

"Lia, it's your turn for the treatment team," says Nurse Wanda in the doorway of the group room.

The Hoodie Heaven gods must have read my mind. I follow her to the roundtable room, room 221. My heart begins to race. My palms begin to sweat, and I feel like the white walls of the hall-way are closing in, preparing to squish me like a bug.

"Are you okay, Lia? Do you need to sit down? I can get you a wheelchair. Just wait right here," Nurse Wanda speaks too quickly for my mind to process all the verbal spillage that was just dumped on my ears.

"I'm okay. I don't need one," I string together the correct syllables and words to get Nurse Wanda to stop, turn back around to me, and hold my arm for support and stability just in case I am wrong and faint.

We walk hand-in-hand into room 221. I sit down as Nurse Wanda pulls out my chair. She has amazing etiquette skills. I respond with mine: "Thank you." I look across the table and do my best to grin wide as Nurse Wanda does so regularly. My insides are screaming at the fakeness I am portraying to the team. I really hope my outsides can play along nicely with my insides. They ask me the same five questions that were asked last week. I reply with similar answers, so I expect similar results.

Dr. Cramer scratches on his yellow legal pad with a red pen. A favorite color combination of Ronald McDonald. After some subtle head nodding from Dr. Cramer and Nurse Wanda, followed by some discreet talking between the others sitting at the table, Dr. Cramer looks up at me and slowly opens his mouth. "We are not able to approve a treatment pass this time. However, if you can show us this week that you are serious about treatment, then we can consider it next week." He lists a set of stipulations because there are always stipulations. Transactional relationships are the only ones that exist in a place like this.

"You will need to participate more in individual and group sessions," he contractively states.

I am speechless. I have nothing to say. I cannot believe that my request is being rejected. I have been doing what they have been asking me to do, haven't I?! I have been listening to these strangers' random requests. I have been squirming and screaming on the inside. But I have shown them effort and agreeance on the outside. How could they betray me like this? How could they continue to keep me away from my family, friends, and Ed? Shouldn't this be illegal? This has got to be unethical. Who can I call for help?

"Mom, Dad, Cole?" I call out, but it is silent. Why can't they help me?

I begin to think about Ed and me at the last track meet. He and I are one. I begin to inhale and exhale as though I am running hard on the track. I start to run in place, get into rhythm with my steps and arms, and breathe. All is calm now. All is good.

"Lia, you need to stop running," Nurse Nancy calls out from down the hall.

Huh? I cannot. Why should I? I've done everything they've asked me to do here, and I deserve this time to pretend I am back on the track with Ed there cheering me on. I am tired of giving endlessly with nothing in return. I pick up my speed.

"Lia, I want to talk to you about what just happened in the treatment team. Are you willing to come sit with me?"

I continue to run, and my breathing gets faster. I zone in on her red cowboy boots.

"Lia, what is something that you notice right now?" Nurse Nancy asks.

"Your boots."

"Good, good. What color are they?"

"Red." I must speed up. The conversational pace is not acceptable to Ed's coaching.

"Good. Can I join you in your run?" she asks.

"I don't care," I gasp.

"Phew. I can't keep up. You are fast."

"It's because of your boots. Try taking them off," I slow down enough to give her some of my own coaching advice. Ed would disagree with me on this one.

"My socks are mismatched. I'll keep them on. Do you mind if we take a break and find a place to sit down?"

"I can't. I have to get to 5,000." I continue to run.

"5,000 what?"

"5,000 steps. Then I can be done."

"What happens if you don't get to 5,000?"

"My dad will be gone forever, and Ed will call me a wimp."

"That makes sense why you feel the need to get to 5,000."

I stop at 1,546. I am shocked that Nurse Nancy doesn't think I'm absurd after exposing my thoughts. This might be the first person I have shared this with who isn't Ed.

"Lia, thank you for taking a break. It seems like it is a very hard thing to do."

"Yeah. But I don't want to stop."

"Yes, it makes sense as to why you want to keep going. Thank you for taking a minute with me. From what you've told me so far, it really sounds like Ed is going to give you a hard time if you stop and do not finish. As well as your worry about your father not staying if you don't finish. Do you agree?"

"Yes. But I am so tired and just want to rest".

"You do?" Nurse Nancy puts her hand on my shoulder, and it feels like a soothing weighted blanket.

"Because I don't do it as much as I used to now that I am here, and Ed isn't."

"Okay, that makes sense. Are you willing to walk with me down the hall and back? We can continue to talk if you'd like."

"Okay," I reply with tears running down my cheeks. I immediately blurt out, "I'm not crying; it's just sweat."

Nurse Nancy holds my shoulder a little tighter, and I immediately feel a calming sensation.

Chapter 12

"Good afternoon, Lia. How are you feeling today?" asks Dr. Cramer as part of his routine opening for our sessions.

"I'm fine," I reply as part of my usual answer to his routine opening. It's a bit of a dance we do. I glance at the white walls and the black-framed diplomas, still neatly hung.

"Okay. Let's try identifying specifically what it is you are feeling. If you'd like, I can pull out the feeling wheel. Just let me know," he generously offers.

"Frustrated. I'm frustrated that I am still here, even after I have done everything you all have asked me to do. I still don't get to go home or, at the very least, get a treatment pass like the others," I grunt back.

"I hear your frustration, and I know that you have been trying to meet your treatment goals. As always, I suggest that you not compare your treatment timeline with that of your peers. Why do you think the treatment team did not approve your treatment pass request yesterday?" he asks, leaning forward in his brown swivel chair.

Because you are all allied against me for no real reason other than to make my life miserable, I want to say. Instead, I keep these thoughts to myself and shrug my shoulders in a polite reply. My mom taught me to always treat elders politely. This is a rule that I can agree to follow if it doesn't include my freedom being involuntarily taken away from me by being locked up here. As a lawyer, she should know how this makes me feel. Yet, the last time I called her, she just kept saying, "Lia, you are there because we love you and want you to get better." She continued to say it repeatedly. It seems she has been attending the family education group here because this is the broken-record technique we are learning in our boundaries therapy group on Thursdays. I have decided that I don't like being on the receiving end of this technique.

"So, you are telling me that you are unclear why your treatment pass was denied. Would you agree with us taking some time to discuss this?" Dr. Cramer asks.

Do I agree? No. But if I disagree, we will have problems with my level of participation or compliance with the program. And from what I am learning about this place, people are here to work on their problems. So, it would be best to avoid adding more problems to my already long list of problems that are supposedly keeping me here.

"Sure," I agree while I glance at the large pile of brown folders with corners of yellow and white papers peeking out on his desk. I wonder if that's where he places his yellow notes with red scribbling when he's done with me.

"Okay, so when you are denied seeing your family and friends on the weekend, you feel frustrated. As I explained to you in the treatment team meeting yesterday, one thing the team would like to see more of is your participation in groups and meals. Do you think that is something you can do more of this week?" he asks as he sits back in his swivel chair, swiveling side to side like he has a nervous tick, awaiting my reply.

"I don't know, maybe," I reply. I feel put on the spot right now.

"Okay, that's a start. How are phone conversations going with family and friends? Have you been reaching out to them during your designated phone times?" he asks as he jots down notes on his yellow paper with his red pen.

"Yes. They have been going fine. Sometimes, I can't get in touch with my friends because they are all busy during my allowed phone time, doing the things that I should be doing." I sarcastically reply as I glance at one of the black-framed diplomas stating Northwestern University in an italic, bold, black font.

"Is there anyone in particular you miss speaking to the most?" He ignores my sarcasm and continues to remain calm while speaking—a foreign experience for me. My mom is the opposite with my sarcasm.

"Of course! I miss Ed," I blurt out without thinking. Man, I've really got to work on my impulse control.

"I understand Ed is an important relationship to you because you have mentioned him in prior sessions. What is it about Ed that you miss the most?" he pries.

"I miss how he helps me feel less worried. I feel stronger with him," I reply.

"It seems to me that your life has had many recent changes, and those can be what keep you wanting to feel in control. Would you agree?"

"Sure. I guess so." I say, placing my arms across my chest—partly because I am cold but also because I feel a bit exposed.

"Well, then, if you agree, I would like to help you find helpful ways to address these recent life changes and uncertainty in the future." His wrinkled forehead and kind eyes tell me that he cares.

"Yes, you can try. But I don't know if it will help. Really, only Ed gets me."

"Okay, I understand. Now, I would like for you to consider what life without Ed would be like." he confidently says.

"I can't. It would be awful. I can't imagine not having Ed in my life. How would I deal with things alone?" I am shocked. Why does he want me to imagine Ed and I not being together anymore? He doesn't even know Ed.

"Ah, I understand. Is there any way you can imagine not being alone without Ed? Having others in your life to support you? Others, who aren't Ed?" He pushes me more.

"I used to have my dad, but now he is gone. My mom is too busy with work and has never really gotten me the way I need her to. My friend, Chloe, has the perfect family, so she doesn't understand why I cry or yell about mine. And my friends in Eat at Joe's band are just people I hang out with. They don't really know many things about me. We just hang out and listen to music. They sometimes smoke weed, but I don't. So don't worry; I don't ingest any substances that alter my judgment. I like to be in control, like I've already told you. Besides, drugs don't help my running."

"How about some of the patients here? Have you begun to feel connected to any of them?"

"Sometimes. I was beginning to talk with Thalia and Zoey. But they left." I throw my hands up in the air.

"I am glad to hear that. They have moved levels and could be a great inspiration for you and the others," he states as he writes more notes down on his legal pad.

"I guess so."

"Okay. So, next week, our session will include your mom and dad. I have invited them in for a family session. Is there anything you would like to discuss before we end for today?" he asks as he begins to put the top back on his pen and put his legal pad down on his desk.

Of course, there is. I wish to discuss why you asked me not to compare myself to my peers here but also recommended that I use them for inspiration. These two thoughts don't match. If this were a math class, Mr. Klaus would draw his big red X on this equation.

I also wish to discuss why we eat so regularly here. I have yet to feel hungry since I was admitted. I am perpetually full. The food costs for the facility have got to be outrageous. Maybe we can have them reduced and invest the savings to make it warmer in the building, but I'd also settle for just getting to wear my hoodie.

I wish to discuss why you think it is a good idea to have my mom and dad in a room together with us to discuss anything other than the weather. Are you aware of the risks of this? I have so many things that I want to discuss with you, Dr. Cramer.

"No," I firmly state as I get up to exit the office which sometimes feels like the principal's office.

Chapter 13

"Good morning. This morning, for the anxiety skills therapy group, we are going to practice abdominal breathing and progressive muscle relaxation to reduce anxiety. Please grab a yoga mat and lay down on your back with your eyes closed," announces Nurse Wanda.

"How are we supposed to lie down after having just eaten so much? I'll get sick feeling my food settle," asks the new admit, Max. Max is about fourteen years old. He speaks his mind, which I find enticing. He is from the city and talks a lot about his dream of being on Broadway one day. If he makes it, I will be there, for sure!

"You will be okay," Nursa Wanda reassures Max and helps him lay out his yoga mat.

"Now, once you all are settled, we will begin."

I hope this isn't another one of those groups where we are led through a detailed visualization of a safe, peaceful place. My brain can't lie anymore. When it's asked to imagine things that are not real for me, it twists into a rage of anger. I despise lying from reality.

"Now, inhale 1, 2, 3. Hold your breath 1, 2, 3, and exhale 1, 2, 3…again." Nurse Wanda encourages us with her soft, hypnotic voice.

This reminds me of when I was younger and tried to hold my breath when my mom was not listening to me. I tried my best to disappear out of a frustrating situation. I felt there was no way out but blacking out. If only my younger self could see me now in this place with no way out.

"Now, tense your calf muscles, then let them go. Good. One more time."

I do as I am told. My calves tighten. My body relaxes, then stiffens like a board when instructed. I am following directions. I'm just not sure what good it is doing me because I still haven't gotten my pass out of here.

"Now, let's open our eyes and slowly sit up. I encourage you to practice progressive muscle relaxation daily and report back to the group on your experience next week. Let's roll up our mats and sit in the circle of chairs for the process group," Nurse Wands instructs us.

We all do as we are told; it's easier to do so. Last week, a new admit (she was only here for one group and one meal; we didn't even get to know her name) did the opposite of what she was told to do, and the staff sent her somewhere else. Where? We don't know. I imagine the answer isn't reassuring.

I sit on the cold, hard, beige folding chair with the other pa-tients. We are all circled, facing one another. It reminds me of playing musical chairs in elementary school, without the music—or permission—to move to. Today's process group therapy topic is for us to begin to understand predisposing causes of anxiety and how we can each relate to them. I try hard to focus and listen to the material being taught because I know we are going to have to discuss it in a few minutes, but I'm having trouble listening when thoughts of Ed are buzzing in the back of my mind. Zoe and Thalia used to refer to this as my "Ed head," meaning I am semi-present with reality but also daydreaming about Ed. I wonder how those two are doing downstairs in Hoodie Heaven. They may even be getting ready to go back home. It makes no sense to me how we live with each other 24 hours a day for days and sometimes even weeks, share our deepest thoughts and feelings with each other, and would still be breaking the rules if we tried to connect after leaving this place.

This type of emotional exposure to peers, and then never speaking to them again, just makes it that much easier for me to stay close to Ed. Recently, Nurse Wanda, Nurse Nancy, and Dr. Cramer have been showing more interest in learning about my relationship with Ed. Part of me is excited to share more of him with them and get them to see how great he is, but another part of me is embarrassed to share some parts about him because then they may not like him. Even though we all know perfection does not exist and we all have flaws, it just isn't the impression of him that I want to share with them.

"Sometimes, people grow up in a family where their parents foster perfectionism, emotional insecurity…" Nurse Wanda goes on, and I drift away.

I don't know why parents don't have to sit through these teaching moments, too. I mean, aren't they also part of the issue? At least mine are. But I don't think my mom and dad see it that way. They just think I need to fix things about myself here, and then, we can all go our merry way. I have felt sad for some time, and now more than ever. Being a teenager who has to be locked up for treatment makes me believe in my brokenness even more. However, I must show my mom, dad, and the staff here that I can be normal.

"Okay, it's time to wrap up process group and prepare for lunch. It's Taco Tuesday," Nurse Wanda announces way too excitedly about the shelled, ground meat we are about to consume.

If it is Taco Tuesday, that means it is also Treatment Team Tuesday. This place is so consistent it diminishes most of my anxiety. If only the real world could operate like this place—but with the freedom to be able to leave when I want, wear what I want, eat what I want, and have Ed here when I want. We are not as close as we used to be since I was admitted here, and this is scary because we are always "we."

"Everyone must wash their hands and then meet me in the cafeteria for tacos!" Nurse Wanda directs the herd of us down the hall, pointing to the bathroom on her right and then the cafeteria on her left.

The cold, white tile floors are as clean as they can be. My slipper socks are losing their grips, making my walks down the hallway more like sock skating. Sometimes, Nurse Nancy tells me to slow down, but I don't mean to go so fast. I know she doesn't understand how sock skating can increase one's speed because she wears her red cowboy boots each shift. I really wish the staff here could see how hard I am working at trying to be normal. I am stuck trying to find a better reason than "because they tell me to" to stop my sock skating, keep eating my meals, go to bed on time, take my medications, and attend therapy. All I can think of is, "Because I can get back to being with Ed all the time."

"Okay, everyone can start eating now. We will stop in 30 minutes," a familiar voice states. It's Nurse Joyce from the emergency room. She is dressed in her Disney-themed scrubs and is smiling big. I wonder why Nurse Wanda abandoned us; she sounded so excited about the tacos being served.

Nurse Joyce speaks about her recent trip to Disney World and how she is still spinning from the teacup ride. I find this hard to believe. Usually, when I am spinning, it's right before I faint. Is Nurse Joyce going to faint? Should I warn her? At least she is seated, so she can't fall too hard. Swallowing my lunch is difficult with lumps in my throat. I feel guilty for not warning Nurse Joyce of her potential fainting, but I cannot stand drawing attention to myself, especially when I am eating. Max joins in about his days spent at Disney World and how Space Mountain made him throw up all over the person sitting in front of him on the ride. I place my spork down. That's it. I am done eating.

"Max, remember that we are to keep the topics of conversation light and non-triggering," redirects Nurse Joyce. She is still sitting up and awake.

"Okay, but it's true," Max replies with a mouthful of food. Gross. Watching others eat disgusts me. At home, I only eat alone or with Ed. I like it better that way.

We hear more about the parades, characters, and magical things that occur in this magical place. I am not impressed, but some of the other patients appear to be invested in hearing it all. I was not impressed when I was five and went to Disney World for the first time. My imagination created a cooler place in my mind, so when we arrived and walked through the gates of Magic Kingdom, I was disappointed. Then angry about having to wait so long for a short ride. Then sad that the souvenirs were too expensive to buy. In my mind, Disney was different. I learned from that point on that I expect too much, which leads to being disappointed regularly.

"Lia, the team is ready for you in room 221," Nurse Wanda whispers in my ear, causing me to jump ten feet in the air and spill my crumbled-up beef on my blue hospital gown.

"Oh no, let me get you another taco, Lia. You can eat in the treatment team room," Nurse Joyce concludes.

I follow Nurse Wanda to room 221, sock skating with a taco in my hand, smelling like a taco truck and cringing at the greasiness and sauce that is causing my blue hospital gown to stick to my legs.

Breathe, Lia. Remember that time your dad gave you a coin to make a wish in the fountain at the mall? You threw it in, but it landed on tails, and you were convinced this meant your wish would not come true. So, you leaned into the fountain and reached for your coin to flip it over to heads, but you fell into the fountain and had to wear your soggy clothes all the way home. If I could sit through that, I can sit through this. Right?

I sit at the table and see the panel members smiling across at me. Each one sitting in the same seat they sat in last Tuesday and the previous Tuesdays. I listen as each one summarizes their thoughts about my progress, or lack thereof, over the past week. I feel judged. As each member goes, then the next to their left, my heart begins to slow down. It sounds like everyone is happy with me this week. Dr. Cramer shares how much progress I am making in individual therapy sessions, which I don't fully agree with, but I won't tell him this. When everyone is done, Dr. Cramer approves me for a day pass this Saturday!

"Okay," I manage to spit out, but inside, I am still choking. I smile big and thank the roundtable crew for approving my pass, and to reassure them that I won't let them down. The pecking order smiles back.

"Please remember that a search will be conducted when you return from your pass, and you must therapeutically process with Nurse Wanda, who will be on shift," Dr. Cramer adds.

"Okay," I agree to this ridiculous request while silently thanking Nurse Wanda for not telling them about that "cheeking" incident last week. I promise to let her check my oral cavity thoroughly and with ease moving forward. I wish Thalia and Zoey were still in blue hospital gown hell so I could share with them all the fine print that came with this pass. I want to be able to make plans to see Ed when I am on pass, but I'm not sure how to do that. I bet Thalia and Zoey could give me some tips from their times on pass. I'll have to find a way to communicate with them.

Chapter 14

"Good morning. Happy Friday! It's going to be a fantastic day!" announces Nurse Wanda from my doorway. As usual, she wakes me before sunrise.

"It's Friday?" I reply, half awake, half asleep. That beautiful place of being in between dreamland and reality.

"Yes, it's Friday. Please get up, get dressed, and join the others in the hall for medication time," she chirps as she waddles away.

"Yuck," I gag. This means it's Family Friday, and I will have to endure a family session today with Dr. Cramer and one or all members of my family. Dr. Cramer gets to choose which member attends weekly based on what he considers to be therapeutically beneficial. Last week was both Mom and Dad, and that lasted for ten minutes before my mom stormed out of the room. My dad said all the right things, as usual, but then could not answer why he wouldn't take me home.

Family Friday also means fried fish and french fries for lunch today to follow the "F" theme. I could think of a few other words to add to this theme if asked to. I take a deep breath and start changing into clean undergarments and a clean hospital gown. Getting "dressed" for the day here is a joke. I leave the room and stand in line at the nurses' station with the others to be dispensed our morning medications. Today, like the other days, I feel stuck in a time loop. Each day is continually repeated, except this morning, I am third in line. Yesterday, I was fifth in line. I must have landed faster into reality this morning than yesterday after being spooked by Family Friday.

"Here you go, Lia," Nurse Nancy hands me a small plastic cup of water and a large multivitamin pill that I must swallow without choking on. They expect so much of me here. I pray fast for my life to not end like this, and swallow and swig the water. It hurts to swallow, but I appear to still be alive. I hand Nurse Nancy my cup and move away for the next person in line to get their turn.

"Not so fast, Lia," Nurse Nancy calls me. Yikes, I thought I was in the clear.

"Dr. Cramer wants you to join him in his office. It's time for your family session," she says as she points toward his office, which is down the long hall.

I sock-skate that way. I hope it is my dad who is waiting for me in room 217 with Dr. Cramer.

"Please walk, Lia. You can fall like that," Nurse Nancy calls to me down the echoing hallway. I stop sock skating and walk instead. She doesn't understand, with her red cowboy boots, how much more efficient sock skating is when getting around this place in sock slippers.

I turn the doorknob to room 217 and see my mom sitting on the couch. I glance at the room to see if there are others for this Family Friday, but she's the only one who shares my DNA in the room. Dr. Cramer is sitting in his brown leather swivel office chair. As always, his fancy framed diplomas hang neatly on the wall, and the bold, italic "Northwestern University" letters remain intact.

"Hi, Lia. Come on in and take a seat anywhere you'd like. As you can see, your mom will be joining us this morning for a session," Dr. Cramer points out the obvious.

I sit on the other end of the couch. There is space between my mom and me. She looks made up. She is one to never leave the house in anything but an ironed shirt and pants, a well-washed head of hair, and just enough makeup to look like she has some on but isn't trying too hard.

"Hi, honey," she says and reaches her hand toward me on the couch. Part of me wants to scoot over and hug her and beg her not to leave me in this place one minute longer. To plead with her to take me home.

"Oh, I must reply to this text before we get started. I am so sorry. It's work." She snatches her hand away fast so that she can begin replying on her phone to the work email she has just received, as if another person's life is at stake if she doesn't do so right now.

All desires to have her save me from this place disappear, and I feel my blood temperature begin to rise to a boiling point. How could she do this to me again? I haven't seen her for weeks, and she couldn't come without her phone for one 45-minute session?

"Mrs. Llyod, as I mentioned over the phone when we scheduled this family session, it is very important for you to refrain from any outside distractions for these scheduled 45 minutes so that Lia, you, and I can get some good family system work done," Dr. Cramer—the man—reinforces his boundary with my mom. Love his bravery with this.

"Yes, I am just about done. I am sorry. I will put my phone on 'do not disturb' after I send this email."

She doesn't care about me. I am locked away in a scary place without any of my own belongings and no privacy. And she doesn't even seem to care about anyone or anything else but her work emails.

"The sooner, the better, Mrs. Lloyd. I'd like to start with you, Lia. How are you feeling about this family session this morning?" Dr. Cramer asks as he shifts his knees, shoulders, and face toward me. He is completely present and engaged with me. So much so I feel a bit uncomfortable. Suddenly, I realize it's because I'm not used to this kind of attention, and I am now questioning why I judged him so harshly all these weeks. He seems to be a caring and genuine person—unlike my workaholic mother sitting at the other end of this couch typing fiercely away on her phone.

"Okay, I am done. Phone is down," my mom interrupts Dr. Cramer's and my bonding interaction.

"What can we do to get Lia to be her old self again, doctor?" my mom blurts out like she has been dying to ask this question for weeks now.

"Mom, I don't want to be my old self. What do you even mean by that?!" I blurt back.

"I just want you to be happy again and hang out with your friends like you used to. You stopped hanging out with your friends in that band. What are their names again?" she asks.

"I didn't stop hanging out with them," I answer.

"Then what happened?" she asks as though she is trying to prove a point and is not actually curious.

"Nobody knows what to say to me about my dad leaving. I didn't stop seeing my friends. They just stopped seeing me," I blurt out without thinking.

Am I too old to run and hide under my bed in room 233? Part of me wants to run and hide like I used to when my mom and dad would fight. Another part of me wants to interrupt my mom from speaking and stomp, scream, and shout until every thought inside me is out. But I know better than to do so with Dr. Cramer in the room scribbling words on his yellow notepad that would later be added to the large brown folder they have on me that is locked in the filing cabinet each night before he leaves with the key in his briefcase.

"Lia, you have got to get over the fact that your dad and I are separated and almost divorced," my mom pleads.

"I don't have to, and I won't. Mothers and fathers are supposed to stay together, be adults, and figure out how to stop fighting with each other. You all expect Cole and I to do the same," I remark.

"Perhaps we can all take a deep breath and let each other calm down before we continue. I know that Lia has been learning de-escalating skills in the group. Haven't you, Lia?" Dr. Cramer interrupts the thick tension that is building between my mom and me.

"Well, I hope these groups are helping. They sure are costing our family a lot of money," my mom adds right before Dr. Cramer stands up and asks her to exit the therapy room with him and into the hallway.

I would give almost anything if I could quickly learn advanced lip-reading skills. All I can see through the small glass on the door is my mom standing in the hallway with her arms crossed and her head looking down at the white floor. I can see her hair neatly parted in the middle and pulled back in a large clip at the base of her neck. Her hair is colored a dark brown every four to six weeks at a place in the mall, but a few gray strands are showing—something one should never point out to her. I did it once a few years ago, and it angered her so much. I am still puzzled as to why she got so angry. Isn't aging something we will all experience if we are lucky enough to survive life that long?

It looks like Dr. Cramer is trying to get a point through to my mom by talking to her and waiting in silence for a response. His lips move, then they stop and stay stopped. She throws her hands up in disbelief and walks towards the nurses' station. I imagine she is using the restroom to check if her makeup and her hair is all in place. As soon as she is out of sight, Dr. Cramer walks back into his office.

"I believe we will need to reschedule our family session with your mom for another time," he shares as he sits in his swivel chair.

"She left? She's not coming back in?!" I am shocked.

"That is correct. She left for today. I am sorry," Dr. Cramer genuinely looked sad for me. I appreciate his empathy, but the last thing I need is for him to think my family is not able to handle me; then, I would have to stay here much longer because of her.

"I am beginning to understand your home a bit more, Lia. It is beginning to make more sense to me why you choose to hold on to Ed, even when there is a part of you that wants to be free from that relationship as well."

Finally, someone is getting it. I am beginning to feel somewhat reassured that I have been working hard to do things the right way here. This way, Dr. Cramer can see that it is not just me in need of treatment and learning new coping skills. I think he is beginning to see that my mom needs them just as much- that it's not just me who is the problem and needs fixing.

"I really can't believe that she just left. Although, it does remind me of the time when I was eight, and we were arguing in the car about something. She got so mad at me. She dropped me off on the side of the road and drove away with my brother in the car. I stood there and wondered how long I'd have to wait for her to come back and get me. It felt like a long time."

Chapter 15

"Good morning, Lia. How are you feeling?" Dr. Cramer asks, per his usual self.

"I'm a bit nervous and a bit sad," I answer Dr. Cramer correctly, this time to avoid his offer to pull out the feelings wheel to assist me.

You're making a mistake! Ed's voice warns me in my head.

"Please take some time to elaborate for me, Lia," he requests.

"Okay. I feel nervous about my upcoming treatment pass because I don't know how my mom will act around me after our last family session. I haven't heard from her since then. And I'm sad that I won't be seeing my dad while on pass because the last time I spoke to him, he suggested it would be best if he stopped asking my mom for visits because it seems to create more stress and drama for us kids due to my mom making it difficult. Is that elaborate enough for you, Dr. C?"

Good, Lia. You reigned it back in. Ed's voice celebrates me in my head.

"Yes, thank you for sharing. That is a lot to process before your pass. I can see why you are feeling nervous and sad." Dr. Cramer says, leaning closer to me in his chair.

"Why couldn't I have just been born into a normal family like my best friend Chloe's family?" I plead to the skies for an answer.

"I know that your family situation is difficult to navigate. How can I best support you in preparing for your pass this weekend?" Dr. Cramer generously offers assistance. But I know that Ed may not be on board with it this weekend.

"I don't know. Maybe investigate ways I can be encrusted with an emotional shield to protect me from the nudges and punches I feel inside whenever I am back home and feel like I cannot fit in." I know that Ed is a shield of mine, but he is also mean sometimes, and I don't like it.

"I can't exactly do that. But I can help you review ways to create boundaries with those around you. How does that sound?"

"Good, I guess," I say as I shiver a bit.

"Are you cold? Do you want a blanket? This brings me to some good news that I want to share with you. This afternoon, Nurse Wanda will be moving you to the first floor. The treatment team and I have decided that you are ready to move up a level in your treatment plan. I know you've been requesting to have your hoodie, and you can have it down there. What do you think?"

"I think this is a very mean joke if you are teasing me about this."

"No, Lia. I am serious. The amount of involvement you have shown the team has been impressive, especially given the difficult family sessions you have had to experience. We see you and support you."

"Oh, wow. Well, thanks. And as far as my family goes, don't worry about it. I am used to them and all that is happening. I'm glad that I have Ed."

"Yes, about that. Can you see how, since being here, you have not needed Ed? Can you see how you have been able to get through your days without him by your side? Can you see how you may want to consider not seeing him in the future and experience life without him?"

"I know you are not a fan of Ed, but he has been there for me when no one else was. When my dad moved out, my mom was busy working, and my brother was out with friends. He has become my best friend since Chloe and I haven't been as close as we once were."

"Yes, that sounds lonely."

"It was. At first, I was annoyed by being monitored here 24 hours a day. But it's grown on me. I feel like you all care. I don't feel that way at home. Only with Ed, minus his dark side, which I suppose we all have."

"His dark side? Can you tell me more?"

"It's not that big of a deal. We all have one. His dark side is just on steroids sometimes," I smile when I say this to reassure Dr. Cramer that I am not in any danger with Ed if that is what he is trying to get at with his questioning.

"Lia, does Ed hurt you in any way?" Dr. Cramer asks in a serious tone.

"No. Sometimes, he is judgmental, but I think it helps me to improve, even if it does feel crummy at the time," I confess. I think this is the first time I've told someone about my not-so-favorite things about Ed. It kind of feels good to let this out. I'm not sure why Dr. Cramer's ears are the ones that have received this instead of Chloe's or Ms. Amy's. I know they both have shown some concern about Ed over the last few months. Maybe it is Dr. Cramer because he is the gatekeeper to the first floor, Hoodie Heaven.

I am beginning to see that this place works in reverse of my normal life outside of here. Here, I am accepted and encouraged to share more when I open up to them. Outside of here, nobody really wants to know how I am really feeling or what I am really thinking. It seems they just want small talk and to avoid digging deeper into my world. And if I do share with them, well, that never goes well. I usually end up having to comfort and reassure the other person that my inner world is not as destructive as they had just heard from my sharing. That I will be okay, and they will not need to worry about me.

"Lia, do you think this is what a supportive and loving relationship looks like?"

"I don't know. I don't have many relationships, and it does seem better than the one my mom and dad have, for sure. So, maybe."

"Can you tell me in what ways he is judgmental of you? Help me understand this better if you will." Dr. Cramer sits at the edge of his swivel chair and leans in to hear me. I can count an additional two gray hairs on his overflowing brows above his eyeglass frames. I hope it is not me and my family who are aging him so quickly. His interest and investment in me make me feel a bit uncomfortable while, at the same time, comfortable. I don't yet know if I like this or not. It may need to happen a few more times for me to know whether I like being paid attention to when sharing. I suppose it is like trying new foods when I was younger. My dad would remind me that it may take several tastes of a new food before my taste buds either accept or reject it. I really wish my dad were here, too.

"Sure. When I got a B+ on my last math test, he told me that I could have done much better if I had tried harder. He told me I should have woken up at 4 AM that morning instead of 6 AM to study those extra couple of hours. I know that he is right and that I should have. I guess I have just been so tired lately, and the previous night, I didn't get to bed until after midnight because I was cleaning my room, doing my daily exercises, and studying for that math test."

"Were you okay with receiving a B+ on the test?"

"Yes. I mean, I was before I saw Ed's disappointment in me. That test was difficult, and I studied for it. I tried my best, and I know my final grade in that class will be good."

"So, what did you tell Ed if you were happy with the grade you received?"

"Nothing. I just agreed with him. It seems it is easier to agree with him than to disagree. I never win when I disagree with him or with most people in life."

"That's got to be hard, always letting others have the final word. What do you do with your thoughts and feelings when they aren't accepted by Ed or others?"

"Nothing. I swallow them. I keep them inside. Sometimes, they eventually come out when I'm on the track running. But I usually feel full of them from keeping them to myself. Eventually, I begin to doubt myself and wonder if Ed is right."

"It sounds like you begin to doubt your thoughts and feelings when they don't align with Ed's. Does he ever tell you that your thoughts and feelings are wrong when they are different from his?"

"Yes, all the time. Which makes me wonder how I even survived life without him. How did I rely on my own thoughts and feelings to get through life if they are this absurd?"

"That is a good question. Are they absurd, or is Ed trying to hijack your mind and heart?"

"Dr. Cramer, that is a big accusation. Hijack?! I don't think so. I mean, maybe he has influenced me a little. But that happens with anyone whenever you spend so much time with them, doesn't it?" I ask as I begin to count the books on his bookshelf.

"It can. But the goal of relationships is to be able to connect with others and feel a sense of belonging without losing your individuality and sense of self. It's a tricky balance. Does this make sense to you?"

"It does." I continue counting. Dr. Cramer sure is a reader.

"Okay. Well, let's get you down to the nurses' station so Nurse Wanda can help you move down to the first floor. We can pick this up in our next session tomorrow. Sound good?"

"Yes. Does this mean I get to wear my hoodie?"

"It sure does," Dr. Cramer replies as we head out the office door towards the nurses' station, which already has a line starting with the other patients requesting their shower items.

Chapter 16

Today is the day. The day I get to spend numerous hours in freedom away from this place. The day that all members of the panel at Tuesday's treatment team meeting finally approved me (after weeks of doing what they wanted: being their puppet). I get to experience life beyond this building for a day. I plan to spend it with Ed. I am excited but also a little nervous if I am being completely honest. Being honest is what I have been brainwashed to do here. Vulnerability and honesty are principles that are highly encouraged by the staff here. In the beginning, I felt exposed and interrogated by the staff, but I am starting to accept and kind of like the genuine interest and concern they have for me and the other teenagers here. It feels weird but also nice to be listened to. Before I sound too much like a sponsored brochure for this place, let me get myself ready to exit those double-locked doors at the end of the hallway!

I stand up from the vinyl beige chair in the recreation room. I am warmer than I have been since I got here because, in Hoodie Heaven, I have traded in my blue hospital gown for my very own sweatpants and hoodie. I am no longer sock skating and admittedly miss it some because my sock slippers were traded for my favorite ankle-length gray socks and Converse sneakers, minus the shoelaces, to make them low-risk. I will never take these items for granted again.

Nurse Ron, a male in his mid-twenties who is built like a machine, gently hands me my personal belongings bag that is kept locked up behind the nurses' station. We only get access to these bags if we are going on a treatment pass or discharging from the hospital completely. Nurse Ron is newer to this side of the hospital. His role here is a lot like Nurse Wanda's role upstairs. His morning wake-ups are not as cheery as hers were, but I don't know of anyone else whose are. Instead of a chirping, "Good morning," along with a wide smile, I get a "Time to wake up! Meet you at the station in five!" He is more efficient and to the point. I am sensing some military background in him, but I could be wrong.

We've been having some fun initiating him to this side of the hospital with some pranks. Thalia, Zoey, and I have been planning ways to prank Nurse Ron since I advanced to this floor. Thalia blushes the most when we get caught by Nurse Ron. I think she has a crush on him. The thing about this place is we know nothing about the staff here, while they know so much about us. We have no idea what Nurse Ron is up to when he exits this building. Does he live alone? Have a family? Does he drive a car? Or take the subway? Is he a night owl or an early bird? I guess that one is answered because he is on the early shift and arrives at 6 AM. Is he a dog or cat person, or allergic to both?

"Here you are, Lia. You can go ahead and change in the bathroom in this hall. Then I will walk you to the exit where your mom will be picking you up. Remember that a search will be conducted by Nurse Wanda when you return tonight. Have a good time," Nurse Ron lists out in a militant way.

"Okay," I reply as I eagerly grab my bag of belongings and head toward the designated bathroom. I close the door behind me. As I open my bag of belongings, I feel my heart beating way too fast. I am not running, so why is it speeding up? I begin to sweat and feel out of breath. My legs feel wobbly. I've been here before when I fainted at school in Ms. Amy's office. This time, I know better. I slide down the wall and sit on the tiled floor near the sink. Think. Breathe. Think of my safe place. Yes, warm beach, sounds of the ocean, smell of suntan lotion, birds squawking… breathe…swish! A tsunami has swept me away…this is not good… not safe anymore. Okay. Breathe. My dad is here…he is holding my hand…we are going to play my favorite video game: Zelda. We are strategizing together. I am safe. Breathe…

"Are you okay in there, Lia? Your mom is here and ready to pick you up," Nurse Ron announces from the other side of the door.

"YES! I am sorry, just handling a womanly situation. I'll be right out," I lie. What?! A womanly situation? I have not had my period since the beginning of summer. Speaking of which, I should let the nurse know. But not Nurse Ron.

"Oh, okay. Do you need me to find Nurse Nancy to assist?"

"Nope. I'm good." I quickly wish I could rewind and unlive the past two minutes of this interaction, but I continue to move forward and unpack my bag of belongings from a seated position on the bathroom floor, too afraid to stand up in case I faint.

I unfold my jeans and sweater that I was wearing on admission to this place. I try to pull my jeans on, but they won't budge past my hips. I don't have time to figure this out. It's best to just keep my sweatpants on and change when I get home.

I slowly stand up and catch a glimpse of myself in the mirror. My brown hair is unruly. It has been hanging in my face for weeks and was finally pulled back with a rubber band after arriving in Hoodie Heaven. My eyes look red and swollen from crying. Breathe…

"I'm ready!" I say with forced excitement as I open the bathroom door to the hallway. I really am excited, but right now, I am more focused on breathing and trying to survive.

"Great. All is good?" asks Nurse Ron.

"Yes," I lie. I can't believe I lied about having a period to Nurse Ron. When I get back, I need to tell Thalia about this. She won't believe it!

I follow Nurse Ron as he leads me to the double-locked doors at the end of the hallway. This walk feels three times longer than it is.

"Lia!" my mom yells. She runs over to hug me as we enter the outside world through the locked double doors.

"Hi, Mom," I reply, my mouth crunched against her shoulder as she hugs me a little too hard.

"Be sure to have her back right at 6:30 PM, Mrs. Lloyd, so Nurse Wanda can do a full check before her shift ends at 7 PM. Have a good time, Lia," Nurse Ron says as the double doors close and lock behind him.

"Let's get you home to shower and change into some new clothes!" my mom shrieks as she looks me up and down.

"Mom, I'm fine. I'm used to wearing these things. Besides, they're pretty comfortable." Of course, my mom is concerned about my appearance. She always has been, while I have not. She and Ed are a bit similar in this way. I guess a shower won't hurt before seeing Ed.

"Cole is away for the weekend with the Warner family. After you went to the hospital, Chloe and her brother reached out to Cole to see how he was doing, and they have been spending more time together. Mr. and Mrs. Warner graciously invited him to their mountain house to do some skiing. Isn't that kind?" my mom asks in a way that doesn't leave much room for a response.

Kind? How is it kind of my best friend, or so I thought, who betrayed me by tattling on me to Ms. Amy, who then called me into her office where I fainted and where this whole mess began?

"Not really. I thought they'd all want to see me," I surprisingly answer her honestly. Therapy is working.

"Lia, don't be like that. This has been hard on everyone. You are away from home," she annoyingly points out the obvious.

Hard on everyone? What about me? The person who is sent away, locked up, and forced to expose my inner world? If this is hard for anyone, wouldn't it be hardest for me?

I think she believes that she and my brother have it harder than I do. This is insane. Is it not? I wish my dad were here to hear all of this. He would understand. Oh yeah, he's gone. Thanks, Dad. Where is Ed? I've got to be with him.

"Can I see Dad today, too?" I ask her and immediately begin to regret these words leaving my mouth. Especially after she shoots me a look that daggers any hope I have of seeing him today.

"Lia, you only have eight hours to be home, and you don't even seem happy to see me. Even after I woke up early to come get you," she complains under her breath about the hour of traffic she experienced and blah, blah, blah.

"Mom, I am. But you know Dad is also half of my DNA, and I haven't seen him since you both left me at the ER," I try explaining to her.

"Lia, your father and I have been disagreeing on how to best help you with your problems," my mom says.

"Imagine that. You and Dad disagree. Isn't a first and won't be a last," I blurt out as I look out the window at the trees and cars passing by on the interstate, wondering how bad of a hit I'd take if I jumped out now and found another way home.

"What is that supposed to mean, Lia? I do so much for this family, and your father is off living his own life. And you don't seem to be able to see that, do you?" My mom slams both her hands on the steering wheel. I'm surprised the airbag doesn't react to this.

"What do you want me to say, Mom? Thank you for being a mother? I didn't ask to be born. You chose to have me. You signed up to be a mother! So deal with me." I am so close to opening the door and leaping out, but the damn child locks are on. Locked up again, but this time in a moving vehicle.

"I cannot believe you! Your grandma…" She continues ranting as I drift off. I cannot hear this right now. I cannot go on hearing her talk about how hard her childhood was and what she had to endure, as though it excuses her from her poor choices or expecting me to empathize with her feelings about my dad. I don't, and I won't.

Ed, where are you? I need you here to survive this ride back home with my mom. Please come save me!

After about twenty more minutes of me drifting away and my mother ranting, we arrive at home. I run out of the car and into my house. The smell is still the same: roses with a hint of toast and coffee. Homey but haunting at the same time. The smell reminds me of my dad's morning bagel and coffee, but he is not here. I wonder how long he must be gone before the smell of him leaves, too. I don't want it to leave. It won't feel like home.

I run up the taupe-carpeted stairs and down the wood-floored hall into my bathroom. Someone has been in here since I've been gone. My face wash has been moved. It is usually on the right side of my sink, and now it is on the left. My toothbrush holder and toothpaste have also been moved to the left side of my sink. Whoever has done this must be left-handed. It would only make sense for this new system.

"Lia, there are feminine products under your sink. Nurse Ron mentioned you may need some today," my mom yells to me from downstairs.

What? Why would I? Oh yeah, I masked my last panic attack as being a "time of the month" incident. Luckily, I haven't had any of that "lady business" for months.

"Thanks, Mom, but I don't need them. He must have been confused with another patient," I snap back to her.

"You don't have your period? We are normally on the same cycle together. How long has it been?" she asks in a nosey manner.

"Months." I slam the bathroom door and jump into the shower to drown out any replies from my mom. I need a break.

Chapter 17

I've been home for three hours, and already, things between Ed and I feel different. We don't feel as in sync as we had been before I was forcefully locked up into treatment. I wonder if he notices this, too. Does he know how much I have been defending him to all the Tuesday Treatment Team panel members? That I only agreed with the panel to get them to approve me for this day pass that now feels like it is not going anything like I had hoped it would have gone?

With Cole being away with the Warner family, my mom being on her phone preparing for an upcoming court case, and my dad not returning my phone calls, I figured things with Ed would be going well since there aren't other interruptions, distractions, etc.

It started with taking a shower. It seemed he was waiting for me too long. But I was sad after standing in front of my mirror and not really recognizing the girl glaring back at me. It appears my brown hair has become extra unruly and needs a trim. My blue eyes look puffy from weeks of early wake-ups and waking up multiple times each night when checked on by the staff. My face also looks rounder than before. I wonder if Ed notices these things and is pulling away from me because of them.

"It's time for lunch," my mom yells from downstairs.

Ed and I head down and take a seat at the kitchen counter. I pull out the bar stool where my dad used to sit every morning, reading the newspaper and sipping on his coffee. Looks like my mom isn't joining us; it's just me and Ed biting away at our egg salad sandwich. I can hear my mom tapping away on her computer keyboard in the other room. It feels weird eating in front of Ed because it's so much different than eating with the others at the hospital. There, we play table games and engage in light conversation, making mealtimes more enjoyable. I complain to them regularly when I am there, but honestly, I miss them a little bit today.

Just like my mom skips breakfast, she often drinks her lunch in a diet shake. I wish she would make me lunch and eat with me the way my dad used to when he lived here. "Lia, make sure you grab yourself some lunch. Dr. Cramer wants me to let him know how you do on pass," my mom states as she walks into the kitchen. She sees me eating my sandwich at the counter on my favorite plate that reminds me of my dad.

"Just wrapping it up, Mom," I half lie. I know that half a sandwich is probably not enough, but I am so uncomfortable with Ed it's all I can stomach.

"Oh, good. Do you want one of my shakes? I've got some new flavors. They don't taste as bad as they used to." My mom offers me one of her diet shakes. I know that she is trying to be helpful, but Dr. Cramer has specifically spoken with her several times about getting rid of these shakes before I come home and sitting down to eat meals with me like my dad used to. Each time, I watched her agree to his direction, yet here we are.

Between Ed and my mom in the kitchen, I feel like I need to run. It makes sense now why I fell in love with Ed; he reminds me of my mom sometimes. In a group Nurse Ron ran this week, he taught us how we can sometimes find ourselves in relationships that are not the best for us but remind us of home. They are familiar. They are with different people, but like the ones we have. I can kind of see what he was talking about.

"Mom, how come Dad isn't returning my calls? Doesn't he know that I am on pass today? I want to see him," I ask her as I get up from the counter and bring my plate to the kitchen sink.

"No, honey. I didn't tell him you are on pass. He has been threatening to get a lawyer to handle our divorce, and I am not okay with that, so I stopped talking to him," she says too casually.

"Do you think I can visit him on my next pass?" I am scared to hear her answer.

"Why? Why would you want to see him? He has hurt me and will hurt you, too," she snaps back.

"Because he is my dad, Mom. What did he do to you? You know what? I don't want to get into it with you. I just want to see him. I miss him." I feel my eyes filling up with tears, so I turn away from her and look out the kitchen window at the treehouse that my dad built my brother and me when we were in elementary school.

"Well, good luck. That man only cares about himself," my mom says as she storms out of the kitchen.

I don't get it. I don't know why she gets so angry with me whenever I bring him up and talk about missing him. He hasn't done anything to me. He is my dad. I love him.

Ed and I decided to go on a bike ride to get out of the house. It's been several weeks since I have gotten to ride up and down the streets of my neighborhood. I retrace my usual route and ride by Chloe's house. As I ride by, I remember that the Warner family is not home this weekend, which means that I can't catch a glimpse of their "family fun time," which is what they call their Saturday afternoon time together. So, I continue pedaling on. Ed pedals fast, so I pedal harder. I am beginning to breathe hard, but I keep going to keep up with him. My legs burn, and I am starting to feel mad that I must pedal so fast to keep up. It seems like no matter what I tell him about slowing down some, he ignores me and continues. Maybe it's me? Maybe I am too slow, and this is a "normal" speed? Am I being a wimp? Shouldn't I just go faster and stop complaining?

"Hey, watch where you are riding, young girl," an older woman with pink reading glasses sitting close to the steering wheel in a white Cadillac yells outside her window.

"I'm sorry," I pant and slam my brakes.

It's time to head home. I almost got hit by a car trying to keep up with Ed. I turn around and head back home. I don't know where Ed went or if he knows I turned around. Right now, I don't even care; he almost got me killed.

I stop in the Warner family's driveway. I stop and stare at their pretty window treatments on the inside and how they match the pink and purple petunias in the flower boxes outside. I want to go inside. I want to pretend I live a normal family life like Chloe. I walk around to the back porch, tilt the big potted lemon tree on its side, and grab the extra house key hiding under the pot. I unlock the back door and walk into the kitchen. It is immaculate, as always. A glass jar filled with homemade chocolate chip cookies and a large silver bowl of apples and oranges. Both are consistently full. It would be concerning for me to find an empty counter. I look around and browse the framed family pictures on the wall going up the stairs. They are staggered when hung and nothing like Dr. Cramer's framed diplomas. The frames vary in size and color, and you can tell they were hung with approximation, not exactness.

I lay down on Chloe's bed, like I have done so many times before, and sink into her soft pillow-top mattress. I feel like I am in the clouds. For a moment, I feel at peace. No more wondering if Ed has noticed that I turned around. No more panic that I almost crashed into a moving Cadillac. No more hour countdown until I return behind locked doors with an interrogation from Nurse Wanda about the day's happenings. I reach my arms over my head and grab one of the fluffiest, biggest pillows I have ever encountered. I grab it and tuck it under my head, feeling something hard and book-like inside the purple pillowcase. I dig into the cloud of the pillow and pull out a little brown leather book. I open it and begin to read without hesitation and gasp and hold my breath on page two. I am holding a book of love letters written between Chloe and Cole. My brother, Cole! How do I know this is my brother, Cole? Because what other Cole signs his name like a five-year-old and writes about the *Back to the Future* Lego set I gifted him last Christmas?

Is this why last year, when Chloe was at my house, she said that Cole looked so handsome as he was dressed in his homecoming tuxedo and getting ready to pick up his date? Has she had a crush on him since then, or even before that?

My heart beats fast while I lie here. I cannot breathe. Am I fainting? Why is the room getting smaller? Dad, think of Dad. He is coming to get me from Chloe's house like he did last year. He picked me up to bring me to my favorite pizza place, Gio's—a small place above the movie theater that only has two tables to dine in, and the rest must be taken to go. But Dad and I are the lucky and loyal diners for whom Gio reserves the table in the corner. We are eating thin-crust pepperoni pizza on red plastic plates and drinking water from brown plastic cups. All is safe. All is good. Breathe. Breathe. My dad tells me some funny jokes that he learned over the years. He tends to tell me the same ones repeatedly, but I laugh every time. The one about the orange—I laugh so hard I spit water across the table, and he doesn't even care that it lands on his pizza.

I hear a door slam and jump to sit up on the bed. I stay still to hear who it may be. Did the Warners come home early from their weekend getaway? Is someone trying to break into the house? I stuff the little brown book of hidden love between my bestie and brother and hide under the bed. After a few minutes, I hear the door slam again, followed by silence. I hope it is safe to leave the cramped area under the bed. I creep down the stairs and don't hear or see anyone. I tiptoe out the back door, closing it quietly behind me. I run to the front, grab my bike, hop on, and head down the driveway, where I see Mrs. Baum, who lives to the right of the Warners. She is carrying her watering can. It must have been her in the home, watering the house plants while the Warners are away.

"Hello," I say as I pedal by her.

She doesn't respond. She continues to walk toward her home with her watering can. I imagine she is hard of hearing or has no desire to interact with me. I prefer not to interact as well.

I ride fast down Crescent Oak Lane, make a quick right, pass Lotus Lane, and then Blossom Street. I arrive back home. My mom is already in the car waiting to take me back to the hospital. I'm not sure how long I was away from the house, but I see that Ed is back here, too. I park my bike on the driveway and hop into the back seat next to him. I hope this ride will be a bit better if I pretend to be napping the whole way back. My mom puts on her Christian music, and we are silent upon arriving back at the hospital.

Chapter 18

"Lia, welcome back. How was your pass? As mentioned, it's time for me to complete a search to ensure you are not bringing in contraband items. Please empty out all the contents from your pockets," Nurse Wanda firmly requests as I walk through the locked double doors.

"I didn't bring anything in with me." To be even more convincing, I turn my pockets inside out to show her nothing but lint balls.

I am exhausted from today. My thoughts are spinning all around inside my head, and I don't know how to make them stop. Things between me and Ed were off. They weren't how things were before I came here. I am glad to have been able to ride in the car with him after reading Chloe's journal. How could I have not known? How could she and Cole do this to me? Ed reassured me that he is consistent and predictable and that I can rely on him. I leaned in closer to him, knowing he was right. How can I ever trust Chloe and Cole again? I am glad I still have Ed, and maybe we can get back to how we were before when I have left this place for good.

"Okay, you are good to head into the dining hall now and join the group for dinner," Nurse Wanda confirms.

I have lost my appetite after today. I grudgingly take one step in front of the other and head that way. I can hear the others laughing at Nurse Ron's stories, and for a second, I feel at home for the first time since my dad moved out. It doesn't make sense. How could this place filled with staff members who are being paid to be here begin to feel like family and home?

Thalia and Zoey saved a seat for me and are eagerly waiting to hear how my day pass went. I'm not ready to tell them what I discovered about Chloe and Cole's secret love for each other. Instead, I ask them to fill me in on today's level two gossip.

"Lia, you should have seen it. Max tried to play the harmonica today in music therapy group, and he was horrendous. He said so himself." Thalia shares through laughter.

"And Nurse Ron let us play games all afternoon instead of having to do cognitive behavioral group because we all completed 100% of our lunch. We missed you in our Monopoly game," Zoey adds.

"Of all the days to have my pass!" I play along with the social skills that match theirs and smile, hiding what I am feeling inside.

Luckily, dinnertime is when the fun and easy table topics come out. They are little white pieces of paper placed in a wicker basket. The staff take turns adding to it. Nurse Ron is excited about his contributions to tonight's meal. I robotically converse, chew, and swallow, not sure what to even feel or think anymore. After dinner, we are scooted towards the group room to practice relaxation skills. I am grateful for this, to lie down on a yoga mat, close my eyes, listen to soft music, and escape into thinking about me and Ed being with my dad. No more having to pretend to the others and the staff. Any hint of sadness, anger, or hurt will set off the staff's alarm bells and result in a one-on-one sit-down talk session of processing. I do not want to do that tonight.

The lights dim, and I follow along with the instructed inhale and exhale. I continue to breathe in sync with the others. My stomach is knotted while trying to digest tonight's dinner, making this an almost impossible task for my digestive tract. Breathe. Think of Ed. Think of my dad. Think of how we all love to bike ride and should go soon. Think of the music Dad and I used to play on our rides. He would make special playlists and surprise me for each ride. He doesn't make me pedal as fast and hard to keep up as Ed does. Instead, we take our time, look around us, talk about school, or how Mr. Pringle organizes the shelves at my job, or how Cole's newest crush blushes at him. Wait! Don't go there. Turn back. Breathe. Ed reminds me that I can get through all of this with him. How can I get closer to him when I am out next? I want things to return to how they were before.

"When everyone is ready to open their eyes, let's do so. Slowly sit up, then stand. When you are ready, roll up your yoga mat and return it to the corner. Then, line up at the nurses' station for nighttime meds," Nurse Ron breaks into my thoughts. This always seems to happen here.

On my way back from showing Nurse Wanda the inside of my mouth to reassure her that I am not "cheeking" my meds tonight, I hear Carl humming a song. It sounds familiar. As he washes the floor, he hums. He looks up at me and smiles. One of his front teeth is gold. I smile back, then head to my room for the night. When I close my eyes, Carl's humming replays over and over in my head until I fall asleep.

"Good morning, Lia. Get dressed, then head to Dr. Cramer's office for your morning session," Nurse Nancy instructs as she sways her long hair over her right shoulder and begins to walk away. I hear her red cowboy boots with each step she takes down the tiled hallway to wake the others.

I wash my face, put on a new pair of sweatpants, and pull over a new hoodie. I switch back to the others each night. On Sunday, they collect our laundry, wash it, and then return it. I am running low on clean items, but I don't really care, either. As I walk down to Dr. Cramer's office, I see Carl again and wave. He waves back. I suddenly remember the song he was humming. It was from one of my dad's playlists he made for our bike rides. It was "Beautiful Day" by U2.

"Lia, come on in," Dr. Cramer barges into my thoughts. They are consistent at doing that here!

I walk through the doorway of room 217 and take a seat across from Dr. Cramer. He is sitting in his usual brown swivel office chair, eager to start the session. He has his yellow legal pad on his lap and a red pen in hand.

"Good morning, Lia. How are you feeling today?"

"Hopeful," I quickly blurt out to avoid the feeling wheel being suggested. I avoid eye contact as well, to prevent him seeing through me, and I focus on the neatly hung framed diplomas instead.

"I'm guessing your treatment pass went well?"

"Yes, it did," I blurt out another lie. I'm beginning to feel guilty. What I really want to say is that my pass was awful. My mom was absent most of the time and did not follow your instructions while eating with me. She's fighting with my dad and wants me to take her side. My dad is not answering my phone calls. My brother and best friend have a secret love. And things between Ed and I are off.

"Great. I checked in with your mother, and she seemed to think it went well, too."

Of course, she did. She is unaware of anything and anybody that isn't her or her job. Of course, she thought the disaster of a treatment pass went well.

"And after reading the notes from Nurse Ron, it sounds like dinner went well. As well as reading Nurse Wanda's notes on how the rest of the evening went."

"Yup." The guilt of lying to this kind man is starting to get to me, but I must continue this path. It is the fastest way to get out. Forgive me, God.

"Great. So, how do you feel about us beginning to set a discharge date? It seems things are going well here. We would encourage you to continue therapy with an outpatient provider and continue your healing once you return home. I think family therapy would also be very helpful. I will let your mother and father know this as well. Thoughts?"

"Are you serious? How soon are we talking? I'd love to get out of here. No offense, Dr. Cramer."

"No offense taken, Lia. I understand you are eager to practice all the skills you have learned while here."

Sure, that's it. I'm super eager to practice my thought-stopping techniques and relaxation activities and continue to ingest various medications, all while trying to be a normal teenager. Not really. I am just eager to be back with Ed and fix things between us so things will be how they were before I came here.

"Yup. I am."

"How about we set your discharge date for one week from today? That way, we can have a couple more sessions with each other and a family session with your father before you leave."

One more week of treatment and a session with my dad. I can do this.

"That sounds good." I smile so wide for the first time in a long time that the muscles in my face shake. They are not used to this position.

"Now, let's take the remaining time in today's session to discuss what school is like for you. You've mentioned it in our previous sessions, but I would like to explore it further since you'll be returning there soon."

"Okay. What do you want to know?"

"Well, what are your friends like?"

"I have—I mean, I had a best friend named Chloe. We had been best friends since the third grade, but this year, we have grown apart. She went behind my back and got our school counselor, Ms. Amy, all worried about me. Which led me here."

"And why do you think your friend Chloe was worried about you?"

"My former friend Chloe? She wasn't. I think she was just jealous about me having Ed. Things began to change once I met Ed."

"I see. Did your relationships with other people change, too, once Ed came into your life?"

"Not really. My mom and dad were already fighting and then separated. My brother was already busy with his friends and no longer liked hanging out with me like we used to. Matt, Joey, Grace, and Sheldon had already been spending more time in Matt's garage practicing for their band and smoking weed. I tried it, and I don't like the way it smells, so I stopped going over there so much."

"It sounds like there were a lot of interpersonal changes in your life around the time Ed showed up."

"Yeah, but it's fine. I just wish my dad didn't have to move out. That one is the hardest to get over."

"I hear you. And I am so glad we have another family session where you can talk to him about this before you are discharged. It is important for you to process this with him. Are you up for that?"

"Yeah, if you can get him to return your phone call. I couldn't get him on the phone when I was on pass."

"I will try my best to get it scheduled. I am sorry you couldn't speak to him or see him during your pass. I'd like us to address this with him in session, too. Anything else you'd like to discuss before we wrap up for today?"

"Nope. I'm good."

"Great. Then, I will see you tomorrow for the treatment team."

I skip out of his office, smile at Carl polishing the floors, and begin to hum "Beautiful Day" by U2.

Chapter 19

"How was your phone call with your father, Lia?" Dr. Cramer asks from his brown swivel chair.

I look over at my dad sitting on the opposite side of the couch from me and smile at him. I look down at my laceless Converse sneakers and begin counting the lace holes on each side of the shoes' tongue. 1, 2, 3…

"It went well," I answer mid-counting. I hope Dr. Cramer can sense my flexibility and how I am trying.

"Did you get any insight into why your father wasn't able to join you on pass?" Dr. Cramer asks as though my father is not in the room with us.

"Yes. Because he didn't want to argue with my mother and cause more stress for me on that day," I reply. I glance over at my father to see if he agrees with this explanation. Did I get it correct?

"I want you to think about the last time your mother and father were in the same room as one another and sit with that picture for a moment."

"Okay," I really don't like where this is heading.

"Next, I want you to think about what happened that day for you. What emotion were you feeling during their interactions?"

"I don't know."

"You may feel uncomfortable doing this, Lia, but that's okay. Can you hang in there with me?"

"Okay," I exhale and look at my dad sitting on the couch with me. I can do this. This is the feeling that usually comes right before I have to call on Ed to help me.

"So, what does that feeling feel like?" Dr. Cramer pushes a bit more.

"It is scary. It feels like I need to run and tell Ed to get out of the room," I cannot believe I just said this. I don't want my dad to think that I like Ed better than him. It's just that when he and mom are together, it gets loud and scary. Ed helps me.

"So, you feel scared? What do you want to feel?"

"I want to feel like I can handle my new life. Life with both mom and dad without having to rely on Ed to feel okay. He isn't always around when I need him, and that is scary, too." I really think this would be nice.

"Lia, I am so proud of you for sharing this with us because now we can work on some tools to get you there," Dr. Cramer responds convincingly, making me believe that what he is saying can be true. "Mr. Lloyd, what are your thoughts on this?"

"It makes me sad to hear, and I want Lia to know that no matter what happens between her mother and me, I will always be there for her," my dad says as he scoots closer to me on the couch and holds my hand.

Chapter 20

"Alright, Lia. Time to gather all your belongings," Nurse Ron gently hands me my personal belongings bag, which is kept locked up behind the nurses' station. It's déjà vu. But this time, I am leaving for good, not just for eight hours.

"Thank you. Is my mom here yet?"

"Yes, she is. She is meeting us outside in the pick-up lane."

Nurse Ron and I walk down the hall, through the locked double doors, and wait for the elevator. As the double doors are closing, I see Thalia and Zoey waving from down the hall outside the recreation group room. I hope they don't lose participation points for leaving the group to wave goodbye to me. The staff had already done a closing circle for me yesterday, where we all said our goodbyes. Both Thalia and Zoey cried. I am not sure why they are still here while I get to leave. One rumor is that my insurance ran out faster than theirs, so I am being discharged first. Another is that they need more treatment than me. We don't know for sure. There seems to be a lot of secrecy around here with the staff, which makes it awkward for us since they expect us teens to emotionally expose ourselves each hour. They hide behind the term "confidentiality," but I think it's just a cover for them to stay a mystery to us.

"And here she is," Nurse Ron rudely interrupts my thoughts, per usual. My mom pulls up, and Nurse Ron opens the door for me. A gentleman, for sure. I wave to him as he closes the door, and my mom and I drive away. I cannot wait to leave the hospital premises for good.

"Honey, we will talk in a minute. I am on hold with another lawyer and have to finish up this call." My mom puts her finger to her lips to remind me not to talk while she is working.

Sure thing, Mom. Don't mind me. I've just been a locked-up teen for many weeks, and now I am finally free, and I am still expected to be silent and contained for you. Fair. Life is so fair.

We pull up to the driveway. I see Cole's red Toyota car parked in our driveway. He must be home. I have not had to see him since I read about his and Chloe's secret relationship. I don't know what I am going to say to either of them. Ed suggested that I don't say anything and keep my feelings to myself. He will help me through this. However, since being in the hospital, it does feel foreign for me not to tell them both what I am feeling. I keep picturing Dr. Cramer's feeling wheel and trying to decide how I feel about Cole and Chloe. I suppose it is just a habit that I had gotten into while there. But Ed is probably right. I should just not say anything.

"Welcome home, Lia!" Cole, Chloe, and the members of the garage band cheer as I walk through the front door. There is a banner hanging that says, "Welcome Back," in blue and red letters, like I had been away at war in the military instead of locked up in a hospital. Something about this all feels bizarre. There are balloons and even a cake. What's next? A clown doing magic tricks? Or making balloon animals? How about a bouncy house? Ed thinks I should smile and say "thank you" to meet the expectations of the guests who came to welcome me back. Since I'm used to relying on him and having him around more, I don't disagree with him.

"Oh, wow!" I make myself say, along with a forced smile.

"We are so glad you are home!" Chloe says while running up to me and giving me a hug. I feel like I cannot breathe. Not because she's hugging me too hard, but because I want to scream at her and can't do so.

"Thanks. I really have to pee." I run off as I lie to my former best friend. I cannot breathe and need to leave her sight.

Breathe. Breathe. Think of me and my dad at my tenth birthday party when we went to a Painting Pottery Café where he painted and gifted me with my favorite plate that has hearts on it. Breathe. Remember how he didn't push me to have a big party every year like Cole had? My mom would push me to invite my whole class to go roller skating, and I only wanted to spend it with my family. Remember how he talked my mom into letting me decide on a party or not each year until he moved out? Breathe. I can get through this. Flush the toilet now to make it more believable that I had to pee. Breathe. Wash my hands for real this time. The hospital always irked me with all the possible germ exposure.

"Lia, is everything okay in there?" Cole asks while knocking on the bathroom door.

NO! Everything is not okay. You and my best friend have been in a secret relationship and still think I have no idea. Mom still doesn't understand me and invited people over for a party, knowing I refused them each birthday growing up, and it isn't even my birthday. It's a party for being released from an involuntary locked hospital stay. And why isn't Dad here, too?! Was he even invited? He knows I was discharged today; Dr. Cramer explained it to him in our family session. I bite the inside of my cheek until I taste blood.

"Yes, it's all good. Just a bit of an upset stomach," I half lie. It's not a complete lie—my stomach does feel in knots and twists.

"Should I get Mom for you?" he asks with a hint of concern in his voice.

Oh gosh, no. She will jump to thinking I'm relapsing if we even mention GI distress to her.

"Nope, I'm good. Coming out now." I quickly turn off the faucet and open the door. I pat him on the back with my wet hands instead of using the Italic L embroidery hand towel in the bathroom that my mom puts out for guests. I want to annoy Cole. I want to make him as mad as he has made me. But he doesn't even flinch. He hugs me instead.

"I sure did miss you, Lia. Now, let's get back to the party!" Cole scoots me toward the crowded living room. I have no idea what is expected of me here. Am I supposed to give a speech and declare, "I am healed!" It's too much to think about. I sit on the white leather sectional couch and pretend to listen to Chloe catching me up on the happenings of the freshmen at our school, but inside, I am floating away. I feel like I have detached from myself and am watching this party as if it were a scene in a movie. I do this sometimes. I like it until I am ready to land and reconnect, but I don't know how. It can be mere hours, days, or weeks before I land.

"Lia, you should have seen the face on Mr. Klaus when his doorknob broke off, and he was no longer able to lock it and keep the late students out. It went on for at least two weeks until the janitor fixed it. Every day, he winced when students walked in after the bell rang." Chloe continues to attempt to catch me up on things I missed at Woodside High School while locked away.

"And Coach Morris kept asking about you. She wants to have you train in the off-season to prepare for earning us another gold trophy next season. She is super excited to have you on the team and kept telling me how much potential you have now as a freshman and that you will only be better as a sophomore, junior, and senior." Chloe stops and looks at me as though she is now noticing my lack of attunement to her speaking about school.

"Are we okay, Lia? I know you were mad at me for telling Ms. Amy that I was worried about you. I know we fought when you were in the ER, and I'm sorry. I don't know how to make it up to you. I only told Ms. Amy because I really was concerned about you." Chloe looks me in the eye.

How could she lie to me like this? I don't believe she was worried about me. I believe she was worried that she and Cole were going to get caught for having their secret romance. So, her plan was to get me locked away and out of sight so she and him could do whatever they wanted without fearing I'd find out.

"Yeah, we're good," I lie. Sorry, God. Lying is getting to be so much easier than having everyone mad at me for saying what I really think and feel. And Ed agrees. He tells me to bite my tongue, which I believe is a figure of speech, but I have found biting the inside of my cheek to be useful in times like these.

"Cake time!" my mom excitedly announces to the crowd.

Ed, help me. Help save me from all of this. I bite my cheek. Are they going to sing to me? Am I blowing out candles? What am I supposed to do at this moment?

"A cake? Of course you got one, Julia. Only you would," my dad states as he enters the front door.

"What are you doing here, David? You weren't even invited," my mom snaps back at him.

"I invited him, Mom. I thought he should be here," Cole speaks up, standing tall and brave while he speaks.

Thank you, Cole, for inviting Dad, but if you are so brave, why not tell me about you and Chloe and your secret relationship?

"Dad! I am so glad you are here!" I screech and run over to him. I normally despise all surprises, but this one, I will take.

"Hi, sweetheart. How about we get out of here? I know you hate these types of things."

"YES!" And just like that, my dad and I leave the party through the front door, hand in hand.

"David, come back here. You can't just take our daughter whenever you want. All her friends are here to celebrate her being home," my mom yells, following us with the cake still in her hands.

"Julia, please go back inside and stop making a scene. It's bad enough you thought throwing your daughter a party after coming home from treatment was a good idea. Now, you want to embarrass her in front of everyone. Go enjoy your cake. I'll have her back by dinnertime. Just be sure to have the house cleared out by then, okay?" My dad speaks firmly to my mom in a way I have not heard before. He must have taken the family education class on communication skills. He is in the assertiveness skills section. Thank you, Dr. Cramer. Your neatly hung, framed, fancy diplomas may be having a bit of an effect after all.

"Whatever. Have her home by 6 PM." My mom stomps away with the cake in her hands, until she turns around and throws the cake at the windshield of my dad's trusty gray Toyota. Then, she slams the front door behind her. I can tell that she is not used to my dad speaking up like this.

Chapter 21

"Lia, it's time to get up for school!" yells Cole from my doorway.

For a moment, that place between dreamland and reality, I picture Nurse Ron dressed in his hospital scrubs instead of Cole dressed in his navy and khaki school uniform.

"Ugh, okay. I'm up." I really want to stay in the purgatory state between dreamland and being awake. It's safe here. I must make it through getting dressed, eating breakfast, drinking coffee, driving to school, arriving at school, and making it into the library for my first period, where I can hide away in the books with Ed and be safe again.

I drag myself out of bed, wash my face, brush my hair, and pull it back into a ponytail. I pull on my khaki pants and navy polo and head downstairs.

I pour myself a cup of coffee, grab my favorite heart plate from the cupboard, make myself some toast with honey, and sit down at the kitchen counter.

"Is that all you're going to have? Don't you think you should have more?" asks Cole, eyeing my breakfast.

"No, I'll grab some more coffee from the teachers' lounge in my first period. This cup should be enough to get me through until then. There's more in the pot if you want some."

"Not the coffee, Lia. I'm talking about your toast. Do you want some of this cereal to go with it?" Cole asks as he pours himself a bowl of cornflakes and splashes it with milk.

"I'm okay. Thanks, though."

"Lia, I'm worried about you."

"Fine, I'll have some. Hand me a bowl." I pour the cornflakes and milk into the bowl. I know I won't be eating it because I despise soggy flakes. And they get soggy quickly. I will finish my toast, though.

"Lia, don't forget to eat breakfast before you leave," my mom yells from the front door as she gathers her briefcase and keys.

"I am. What do you think I am doing? Besides, since when did Julia and Cole Lloyd add food police to their resume?!" I yell back in her direction.

"Lia, don't call me by my first name; it's disrespectful. I'm your mother. I'll be home late tonight. There should be enough food left over from your party, Lia, for dinner. Have a great day back at school," my mom says as she opens the front door.

"Wait a minute. Aren't you driving us to school?" I ask, but she has already left.

"I'll drive us. Mom got me a car while you were away," Cole casually chimes in.

"What? You have your own car, and I'm just now finding out about this?!" I choke on my toast and must take a swig of coffee to save myself.

"Yup. I guess Mom felt bad for me to be the only child while you were gone. So, she gifted me the red Jeep in the garage. Pretty cool, huh?" Cole says with a bit of a bragging tone.

What? Is this real? How has my brother, the guy who has just about everything a high schooler could want and need in life, been gifted a car while his sister was involuntarily locked up in the hospital? My mom felt bad for him?! Hello?! What about feeling bad for your daughter, who was freezing every night for weeks, being forced to wear a blue hospital gown in a place where they refuse to spend money to keep their furnace running well? Or who never had a good night's sleep because of the nightly rounds the nurses would do. Or the fact that I was forcefully kept away from Ed while Cole got to secretly be with my best friend, and neither of them told me? I think I'm the one who should be given something!

"Relax, Lia. Or else you'll choke," says Cole in an oddly chill tone. Does anything even get to this kid?

Have you ever actually seen someone relax when you tell them to? No. It doesn't work like that. Breathe. Think of the time you and Dad took that road trip in his trusty gray Toyota—the one that still has manual roll-down windows. Remember how we went to visit his parents in Florida. Remember the song "Ballerina Girl" playing on his radio. Remember how we would stop and eat at the truck stops and meet people from all over. Breathe.

"Let's go, Lia! Or we are going to be late," Cole annoyingly interrupts my thoughts.

"Okay, okay." I grab my backpack and head out the door.

"Oh, and we've got to stop by the Warner house to pick up Chloe on the way," Cole casually adds into our morning.

As we drive to pick Chloe up, Cole and I are awkwardly silent. I listen to his Spotify playlist, and my insides throw a fit. I cannot get my words out. I want him to just tell me the truth. Tell me that he and Chloe are dating.

"Hi, guys! Thank you so much for picking me up. Lia, it is so nice you are here, too," Chloe says as she climbs into the back seat of the Jeep.

Cole looks at me as though he is trying to read my thoughts about this pick-up. Or maybe he was expecting me to be the one sitting in the backseat so he and Chloe could be love birds in the front. I feel like I am crawling out of my skin. I look out the window and see Mrs. Baum in her yard. I duck low in the front seat to avoid being seen. Did she see me the other day leaving the Warner house? So far, nothing has been said.

"Lia, are you okay?" Cole asks.

"Yup. Just grabbing my bracelet that fell off." The lies are getting easier for me. I would normally feel guilty about this, but reminding myself of the secret love relationship sitting in this Jeep helps me not feel so bad.

As we pull up to school, I feel sick to my stomach. I have not missed Woodside High School since I left. The crowded hallways are hard. The hallways at the hospital were nearly empty, except for Carl making the floors shine. Breathe. Remember the time Dad and I went shopping at the mall for Christmas gifts, and the crowds were so big that Dad wouldn't let me let go of his hand?

Breathe. I walk through the sea of uniformed students until I get to the library. It is quiet. There are shelves of books and an organized system to keep them that way.

This morning, there are not many books to reshelve. So, I grab my self-promised cup of coffee and head to the back of the library, where I can sit at a table in the corner and think uninterrupted. I look at the clock on the wall; it states 8:15. I bet Thalia and Zoey are just now finishing breakfast and heading to the group therapy room for cognitive behavior therapy group. Ed seems annoyed by my reminiscing of my days locked away. He doesn't think the staff there were supportive of our relationship because they did not allow him to be there, too. I missed Ed while there, but now that I am here with him and back home, I find myself missing Nurse Wanda, Nurse Wendy, the treatment team panel, and the other clients. Things there were predictable and always ran on schedule. Not like here, climbing into the red Jeep gifted to Cole by Mom. The nurses always asked me how I was feeling, and there was always someone to talk to. Here, I spend a lot of time either alone or with Ed.

It's almost time for math class, which I am thankful for. Ed also loves math, so I know he will be less pestering for at least an hour. As much as I love our time together, sometimes it does feel overwhelming to have him around. I feel like he is constantly sharing his thoughts and is very opinionated, even when you don't ask him. But I put up with it because it's been nice to fill the silence of Dad being gone. And now that Chloe and Cole are both keeping a big secret from me, I don't really have them, either. Maybe I should catch a band practice in Matt's garage to hang with Joey, Grace, and Sheldon. It's been a while.

The rest of the school day drags by longer than the days at the hospital did. There was a time in English class when I was wishing to play a game of Monopoly in the recreation room instead of reading *Of Mice and Men*. I avoided lunch because I didn't want to fake it with Chloe, who I used to sit with. Ms. Amy offered to have me sit in her office for lunch, but that just feels too weird. I have no idea what we would talk about. It's not like she will have created the conversational table topics like the staff at the hospital did. We would probably sit in silence and listen to my chewing. Or she would probably want to interrogate me again about how things are going at home and school. And I would be so nervous about possibly fainting again and all the unfortunate events repeating themselves. I cannot go back to the scene of the crime, the starting line for it all.

Speaking of starting lines, I've also been dodging Coach Morris since returning. I am thankful for Chloe giving me a heads up at my welcome home party about Coach wanting me to keep training off-season to come back stronger next season, but I really don't feel like having people relying on me—a whole team of my peers relying on me. And I really don't want to encourage Ed to tell me to run harder and faster. When I was on my treatment pass, our bike ride did not go as happily as I had hoped for it to go. I know he wants me to improve as an athlete, but he doesn't understand that I am trying my hardest, and it seems like it's never enough. He truly believes I can and should do more and do it faster. I look like a quitter and a wimp compared to him. I don't even want to lace up my sneakers anymore.

The dismissal bell rings, and the flood of navy-and-khaki-dressed students takes over the hallways, sidewalks, and parking lot of the school. I run to the closest girls' bathroom and hide in one of the stalls. My plan is to wait until the halls empty out. If I miss my ride home with Cole and Chloe, I'll walk home. Ed would choose walking home over catching a ride, no matter the weather. So I can always walk with him.

"Oh my gosh, Chloe, did you see how Cole was looking at you in the hall just now? He is so in love with you. Everyone can see it!" screeches a girl named Violet.

"I know! Although, I don't think his sister, Lia, has been able to figure it out just yet. We have decided not to tell her yet because she's so fragile. We don't want to upset her," Chloe says.

"Yeah, you wouldn't want her to end up back in the hospital again," Violet says.

I pull my feet up onto the toilet to hide even better while in the stall. I bite my cheek hard to keep tears from forming. First off, why is Chloe even speaking to Violet? Violet has been mean to me since the seventh grade, and Chloe and I had made a pact to stay far away from her. And second, I am anything but fragile. The tears that I am trying to fight back are because I don't like liars. Besides, Dr. Cramer always says that feeling my feelings is a sign of real strength.

"Let's go before Cole starts to wonder what happened to me," Chloe says as the two girls leave the restroom.

I'll tell you what happened to you, Chloe. You changed. I don't even know who you are anymore.

Chapter 22

"Lia, it's time to go. Dad will be here any minute to pick us up," Cole rushes me, like always. I don't seem to move as fast as he'd like, so he appears to be constantly annoyed with my speed through life. Usually, I am ready ahead of time when Dad is coming to get us, but last night, I did not sleep well at all. It's been several weeks since I've had a night nurse check happen in the hospital, and I am still waking on the hour, thinking someone is at my bedroom doorway. Sometimes, it feels eerie, and other times, comforting when I wish there was someone checking in on me. To see how I am doing. Taking time out of their own day to be interested in my well-being.

Mom has been busy with work, as always, and has even started going on a couple of dates with a guy named Phillip. He seems dull and nothing like my dad. It infuriates me that she's not even divorced yet. My blood boils every time I think of her putting her needs before everyone else. Why would she do this to us? To Dad? Phillip is a veterinarian, and Mom goes on and on about how intelligent he is. Does Phillip know that Mom has never allowed us to have a pet, like ever? He will find out soon enough.

"Yay! He's here!" I happily shriek as I see Dad's trusty gray Toyota pull up on the driveway. I wave at him from the front window. I bet he's hesitant to pull up in case my mom and any more cakes are nearby.

I run out the front door and yell, "She's not here. It's all safe."

He winks at me and turns his car off. He gets out and gives me a big bear hug. These never get old. Cole comes out and fist pumps with Dad. They have done this for the past ten years. I imagine it will continue for life.

"Where do you kids want to head to today?" Dad excitedly asks us.

"Shoot some hoops?" Cole contributes.

"Head to the mall and people watch, like the old times?" I contribute.

"How about we do both?" Dad says. He always knows how to keep the peace.

First, we drive to the basketball court in the neighborhood park. We begin warm-up by running the court from side to side. Next, it's time to divide up the teams. Because of Cole's height, speed, and dribbling coordination, he plays solo, and Dad and I team up. We dribble, block, run, and shoot baskets. Things are going so well, except for the fact that Cole's cell phone continues to alert him of incoming text messages, which throws me off my game. Ed would play, too, but I didn't invite him today. Honestly, he's been getting more annoying lately—which I imagine is happening because we have been spending almost every waking hour together for the past several weeks since I left the hospital.

"Let's take a water break," my dad says breathlessly as he walks over to the bench.

"Sounds good to me!" I second the notion and follow him.

Cole walks over to check the hundreds of text notifications he missed while we were playing. I have my phone, but the only people who have called me since leaving the hospital are my dad and sometimes my mom when she needs to vent to someone about my dad or her newest case at work. I mostly just listen during those calls. Mr. Pringle also called a couple of times to ask if I plan to return to my bagging job at his store anytime soon.

"Lia, how has school been going?" my dad asks me as beads of sweat drip down his face.

"Not good. Chloe has a new best friend. My classes are moving so fast, and I'm still not done with making up all the work I missed while I was in the hospital. I know the school said they won't count it against my final grade, but it's so hard to know what is happening when I missed so much," I spill it all out without thinking first. The only person I do this with is my dad.

"That's gotta be tough. Do you want me to call Ms. Amy and see if I can help?"

"No, it's fine. I'll get it all done." I must get it all done. I cannot risk another meeting with Ms. Amy.

"Okay, but let me know if you change your mind," he reassures me.

"Hey, can I ask you something?" I spill out again.

"Of course you can, Lia."

"Why haven't you been coming every weekend like I thought you'd be? And why haven't you answered the phone when I tried calling you from the hospital? Did I do anything?"

"Nothing at all, Lia. I am sorry that I did not come to see you every weekend as promised and was not available to answer your calls. I've had a lot on my plate. The separation has been hard on me, and I've been trying my best to get out of this depression. I never thought my family would be divided like this. I know it's no excuse; I should have been there for you."

I can see tears welling up in his eyes. "It's okay, Dad." There is a long pause as we sit in different pools of hurt. He places his hand on mine, and I place my other hand atop his, building a pile of reassurance between the two of us.

He sighs and adds, "I've also been offered a new position at work, and I am trying to decide if I should take it or not."

"That sounds huge, Dad! You should totally take the new position!" I immediately give him my version of a bear hug.

"Thanks, Lia. But the new position is in Chicago," he says, holding me tighter.

"What? Are you thinking of moving there? Leaving me here? You can't do that." I begin to cry and plead. Immediately, I want to take back my congrats and explain all the reasons he can't even consider taking this new position being offered.

"I know, honey. That's why I haven't decided yet. I wanted to talk about it with you and Cole. Your mom knows about it, and she seems so busy with work lately and now that guy, Phillip, but I'm surprised she hasn't told you."

"You mean Dr. Doolittle? Dad, don't worry about him. I don't think it's serious. She'd tell us if it were, wouldn't she?"

"I don't know, honey. Your mom mentioned him a lot at your hideous welcome home party."

"How about we shoot a few more hoops and then head back? I've got to shower and meet up with some friends. You guys can do the mall people-watching things without me. Cool?" Cole interrupts the intense conversation that is happening two feet away from him. He had been busily texting, taking selfies, and calling whoever he disappeared from for a whole thirty minutes because he was spending time with me and our dad.

"Sure thing. Lia, we are still on for people-watching, right? Now, let's go score some points on Cole!" He high-fives me and runs back to the court with Cole.

I feel sick. My head is spinning, and my stomach is in knots. There is a large lump in my throat that is blocking my airways. Am I dying? I can't die like this. Not here. Not now. Breathe. Remember that time when Dad and I went to the basketball game at Cole's school? It was only Cole's school at the time because I was still in middle school. Nope, this isn't going to help me today. Things are looking blurry. There's ringing in my eyes, the voices of Cole and Dad are muffled, and now everything is dark.

"Lia, Lia, wake up," my dad is frantically yelling in my face, and I am not sure why.

"You fainted again, Lia. You are worrying us," Cole fills me in on what happened and is somehow able to make me feel guilty for losing control of my autonomic nervous system, which not one human on the planet can control!

"I did? I'm fine."

"Lia, you hit your head hard on the court when you fell. We really need to get it looked at. Does it hurt at all?" my dad says in a serious tone.

"A little, but I'm probably fine with just some ice," I wince as I touch the right side of my head.

"That's it. Let's go. I'll drive us to the hospital," my dad says as he helps lift me from the court.

"No, not that place again!" I beg.

"Just be glad you're arriving in Dad's car and not the ambulance this time. It's less dramatic this way," Cole says as he laughs.

I know he is just trying to help me feel better, but it hurts to laugh, and I don't find anything funny about this situation. Besides, doesn't he have to get home to shower and meet up with people? What is he even still doing here?

When we arrive at the hospital, we enter the double doors of the emergency room. Since my injury involved me losing consciousness, I'm triaged to the front of the wait. I was hoping to have enough time in the waiting room to convince my dad and Cole that I am fine, and we can continue with our plans of people-watching at the mall.

My dad must have been reading my mind. He says, "Hey, how about we do our people-watching here instead?" as he glances around the hospital's waiting room at the various people waiting.

"No thanks, Dad. I just want to wait."

"Should we call Mom?" Cole asks as the loyal son he is to her.

"No, please don't. I'm fine." I plead.

"We have to, Lia. Cole, I'll call her," Dad calmly states. Sure, he's calm now, but just wait until that phone call ends. His energy will shift.

"Lia Lloyd?" calls a familiar face dressed in pink scrubs with Disney princess faces on them. Is that? Can it be?

"Nurse Joyce? Hi. I'm here," I say as my dad holds my hand for the walk to the nurse.

"Hi, Lia. You remember well. Let's get you to the back and ready to be seen by the doctor. Can you tell me what brings you in?"

"My dad brings me. I'm fine. You can save yourself the paperwork and send me home now," I reply.

"Lia, be serious. Nurse, she fainted while her brother and I were playing basketball with her at the park. She was out for a couple of minutes but then woke up. We saw her hit her head on the ground during the fall." My dad is a traitor at this moment, selling me out to the medical staff.

"Okay, thank you for that information, Mr. Lloyd." Nurse Joyce tag-teams him with a thank you and smile. I've got to get out of here.

"And she hasn't been eating and drinking as much as she did when she first left the hospital," Cole adds. Why is he still here? Why isn't he out there living his secret romance life? And since when was he hired to be my food police? He has always been a tattle-tale, but this is taking it to another level.

"Really, Lia? I had no idea. I can't believe I didn't know this. Could that be why she fainted?" My dad begins to pace. His face is getting red, and his eyes are welling up.

"How would you know, Dad? You don't live with us anymore," I mumble.

"Could be, Mr. Lloyd, but I don't want to say for sure until the doctor examines her. Let me bring her back and get her settled. You two can get something to drink or use the restroom. I'll come get you in a bit." Nurse Joyce takes my hand and holds me up, leaving my dad and Cole to roam freely. How lucky for them.

"I'm going to call your mom, Lia. We will be back there in a minute," my dad reassures me that he is not going to roam in his freedom for too long. He is considerate like that.

"Okay, Lia. You know the protocol. Get dressed in this gown— it opens in the back. And put on these sock slippers."

"Yes, sadly, I do. Do I get a spork, too?" I say sarcastically.

"Sure. Are you hungry? What can I get you to eat and drink?"

"Nothing. It was just a joke I was trying out. Guess you have to be the one in the gown getting pricked and tested to think it's funny."

"Okay. Dr. Whittaker should be joining us soon. Do you remember him?"

"Yes, how could I forget him?" I snap back. He's the guy who started this whole hospital experience and introduced me to the rest of the treatment panel staff. These faces are tattooed in my brain.

Nurse Joyce pulls the privacy curtain shut and disappears into the hall.

Chapter 23

"Good morning, Lia—time to wake up!" says Nurse Wanda from my *new* room 237 doorway.

This time, I'm four doors down from my old room, 233. The rooms look identical, but this one feels different. It seems a new patient named Emerson is in my old room. She's been here for a couple of weeks. I wonder if she's seen the "LL" carved in the bedpost. I used the end of a bobby pin to leave my mark behind. Never did I expect to be back.

I get out of bed and tug on my sock slippers. I dress into a new blue gown, fold the one I slept in, and put it under my plastic-covered pillow. This pillow wakes me every time I move. It crinkles. It gives me a glimpse into what living in a real-life Barbie dreamhouse would be like. I question my eight-year-old self, who dreamed of living in that pink plastic mansion.

I sock-skate my way down to the nurses' station as ordered. I skate by Carl and wave. I wonder if he recognizes me. I recognize his humming and singing. How embarrassing that I am back here. He probably thinks I can't survive in the real world. I can. I promise. I was a Girl Scout. I just haven't been having the best of luck lately. My ex-best friend and brother are in a secret romance, and my mom is dating a vet before she's even fully divorced. And probably even engaged to him if Dad's assumptions are true. And my dad may be moving away to the Windy City, leaving me alone here on Long Island.

And I have no idea where Ed and I are headed. I tried hard to be close with him again after I left this place, and it worked; we got close. But there were times I felt so annoyed, frustrated, and trapped by him. I felt like I couldn't breathe around him. Things are changing between us again, and I am okay with us taking some space.

"Lia, here are your meds. Dr. Cramer will meet with you this morning. So, when you are done here, you can head down to his office. Do you remember where it is? Room 217," Nurse Nancy says as she hands me the small plastic cup with a variety of pills of all shapes, sizes, and colors.

I grab the cup, pop the pills, and swallow them with a swig of water.

"Okay. Now open!" she instructs.

Since when does Nurse Nancy check for "cheeking?" I thought that was only a Nurse Wanda thing. Things have changed around here since I've been gone. But not too much because she's still wearing her red cowboy boots.

With my jaws open wide, she looks in.

"Ouch, Lia. What are all those marks on the inside of your cheek? We need to get you an oral rinse ASAP." She takes a note on her clipboard, and I turn away and head to room 217. I know where the notes on that clipboard go next—they make their way into our medical charts, which they love for each staff member to have access to and read. Again, the staff here can know so much about us, yet we know nothing but the clues we string together and the stories we create about them.

I sock-skate my way to Dr. Cramer's office. His door is open, and he is waiting for me while sitting in his brown swivel office chair. His fancy framed diplomas are still neatly hung. He is holding his yellow legal pad, red pen, and the laminated feelings wheel, in case I need it.

"Good morning, Lia. Come on in." His bushy eyebrows hang over the rims of his eyeglasses. He smiles at me in a comforting way, but I am not comforted.

"Hi. I'm feeling angry," I quickly inform him before he offers the feelings wheel.

"I imagine. Can you tell me more?" he asks as he sits back in his chair and prepares himself to begin taking notes on the legal pad.

How does he hold that pen and not doodle as I talk? He must really be interested in what I have to say. The temptation to doodle would be too high for me. I appreciate him appearing interested. It makes it easier for me to share.

"I don't want to be here again, especially on this floor, without my hoodie and sweats as an option. Why am I here? Nobody downstairs would tell me why. They just avoided my questions, and that makes me angrier," I grunt.

"That would make me angry too," Dr. Cramer agrees with me, giving me a little glimpse into who he is. I appreciate this.

"I can't sit through the groups again, Dr. Cramer. Please don't make me do it. All my friends are gone, too. Everyone here is new, and I don't like meeting new people," I plead.

"I hear you, Lia. I encourage you to give the groups a try. Even though they may be reviewing previous material for you, it could be different based on having new peers' input and you using your time at home to unpack it all and discuss where you used the skills learned and where you didn't. Does that make sense?"

"It does, but I can already tell you that. I used some of the skills I learned, but there is just so much happening around me, and it became too much."

"What became too much, Lia?" he asks gently.

"Life," I whisper.

"That is a very difficult place to be."

"More difficult than me being here again?!" I say, smiling.

"Yes, most definitely." Dr. Cramer does not allow me to try to change the subject with humor like I try so hard to do. "What is it in life that feels like too much?"

"Well, remember my best friend, Chloe? We aren't friends anymore. She thinks we are, but we are not. She and my brother, Cole, have secretly been dating, and no one is telling me because they think I'm too fragile. My mom is dating while still being of-ficially married to my dad. There is some possibility she's even en-gaged. My dad is sad and has been offered a new position at work, which he completely deserves. But it's in Chicago." I list everything off to Dr. Cramer to help him understand what I mean by my life feeling like too much.

"WOW. That is a lot, Lia. I can understand why you feel this way about your life now. Thank you for sharing. I know that you do not want to be here again. I do. Do you think while you are here, we can unpack all this a little at a time so that when you leave, maybe life won't feel like so much again?"

"I really don't want to."

"I hear that. Perhaps we can give it a try? How about you think about it and let me know when we meet again. I plan to meet with you three times a week, like before, but this time, all sessions will be just you and I."

"So, no more family sessions this time?" I ask to clarify in case I am hearing this wrong.

"Yes, that's correct. We won't be doing family sessions this time. What do you think about this?" he asks me.

"I guess it's okay. I mean, you are an expert. So, whatever you think." But inside, I am relieved. It's not like the changes at home that Dr. Cramer recommended were being made.

"I appreciate that, Lia. But the real reason I am choosing to do this is because I want you to focus on feeling empowered to take care of yourself, regardless of those around you. To stay healthy when others around you may not be doing the same. How does this sound?"

"Sounds good. You know, my dad did seem to get something out of the family education series. Can he still attend those? My mom did not follow through on what was asked of her. I don't think she'd attend a second time, anyway."

"Sure. I will give both parents a call and invite them to those classes. I will also explain to them why I am taking family therapy off the table this time. I want you to learn to heal, regardless of others not changing."

"Yikes, good luck with those conversations, Dr. Cramer. I do not wish to be you right now, even if it does mean you get to leave this place and return home tonight."

Dr. Cramer chuckles. I got him to chuckle!

A warm fuzzy feeling comes over me for a second. It is the feeling of home. I know it's not on the feeling wheel, but it's the only word that describes this feeling. I shake it away because I am not home. I am in a hospital with staff. I close his office door behind me and sock-skate to the group room for the mindfulness group. It is Meatball Monday in the cafeteria, which means "M" is the theme.

I grab a seat in the group room. As I remember, the chairs are cold and hard in these blue hospital gowns. They only feel bearable when you get to level two: Hoodie Heaven. Our chairs are in the circle. They always are. A spectator would think we are gearing up for a game of duck, duck, goose or musical chairs. But instead, we are teenagers who barely know each other and are all staring at the ground, trying not to stare at the others in the circle, waiting for Nurse Nancy to begin the group. It is awkward. I feel awkward. But this is taking awkwardness to a new level.

"Alright, we have a full group today," Nurse Nancy says as she slips into the room with her red cowboy boots on. How does a person stay so cheery?

Please don't point me out. Just let me blend in with the other blue gowns in the room.

"Everyone, let's welcome our newest addition, Lia," she announces to the group as she takes her seat.

Darn, I really hate this part of being in the world. The eyes—fourteen of them, to be exact, one pair per seven people—all stare at me. My skin itches and burns. I smile, not necessarily because I want to be polite, as my mother tells me to do when meeting new people. I really hope that I can breathe better. It doesn't seem to be working.

"Okay. I want everyone to get comfortable in their chair and close their eyes."

Phew. Thank you for moving on, Nurse Nancy. Was my face that red from embarrassment? Because you have saved me from the many stares, I'm not even going to challenge your request for us to get comfortable in these very uncomfortable chairs.

"Now, inhale, one, two, three. Pause, one, two, three. Exhale, one, two, three. Pause, one, two, three. Again," Nurse Nancy calmly instructs.

I skip the pausing parts. Holding my breath makes my heart beat faster, and I need to stay calm. I need to pretend that everything is okay. That I am normal. That I can go home now.

"Can we skip the pause? It makes me anxious," a girl with beautiful, straight brown hair quietly asks. I open my eyes in awe of the brave soul that says out loud what I am thinking. She looks at me. Her blue eyes are sparkling. She smiles. I have seen her before, but not sure where. I shut my eyes.

"Yes, Emerson. You can create this in ways that work well for you," Nurse Mary replies.

Emerson. That is who is in my old room, 233.

"Now, continue doing this. In addition, I want you to think of five things you hear at this moment," Nurse Mary instructs.

The clock is ticking. The air conditioner is humming, although it really should be the heater in a place this cold. Wait! I have seen Emerson before at my school. She goes to Woodside High School! She was the one standing at her locker with Ed! The only girl in the school that wears our semi-uniform like a J. Crew catalog model.

Chapter 24

I made a quick friend during treatment this time. Emerson and I met when we were assigned as partners in a trust fall exercise. It didn't take long for us to come up with a plan to break into Dr. Cramer's office.

"Lia, are you sure this is a good idea? I don't know if we should be doing this." Emerson tensely asks as I try to complete our mission while also keeping her calm.

"Yes, it's going to be fine," I tell her convincingly while also trying to convince myself.

"How much longer will you be? Any minute now, Carl will start polishing the floors, and Nurse Wanda will be doing her routine checks on us."

"I know. I know. Remember, this isn't my first time being here. I know the rhythm of the staff. I've watched them closely over time, and I know that this is the only time when there is less of a chance for us to be observed breaking into Dr. Cramer's office due to shift changes," I reassure my partner in crime.

"Okay, but please hurry. I'm supposed to be moving to level two this week, and if we get caught, that will not happen."

"I'm hurrying. I've almost got it," I struggle to get the bobby pin to pick the lock easily, the way the YouTube video walked me through it. Why do those tutorials always make things look easier than they are?

CLICK.

"We are in. Hurry. Quietly close the door behind you," I direct Emerson as we crawl through the doorway of Dr. Cramer's office.

"Remember, let's get what we came in here to get and leave quickly," Emerson reminds me as I begin to slightly move the neat, fancy framed diplomas to a slightly crooked stance.

"What are you doing, Lia? He is going to notice!" Emerson says, way too frantic for this moment.

"It's fine. It's just a small prank. So, where do you think he leaves the key to the filing cabinet? We need to get in there to read all those yellow legal sheets of paper he writes on us," I change the topic to the real reason we are standing uninvited in his office.

"I'll check his desk drawers; you look around in his jacket pockets and wherever else a small key would be kept," Emerson instructs.

I can tell this is her first time being in someone else's place uninvited. Her hands are shaking, her voice is shaking, and she's beginning to panic. I am not new to this. I have a more proactive stance on life. I don't passively wait for an invitation to where I want to be; I proactively invite myself.

"Aww…how cute is this?" I ask Emerson as I hold up a silver picture frame with a wallet-sized boy who looks to be around age two if I had to guess.

"I wonder if that is his son?" Emerson asks.

"Nah, I bet it's his grandson. Have you seen the aging lines on Dr. Cramer's face and the gray hairs on his head? Although, I could be wrong. It could be his son. How are we going to find out?" I ask, debating if we should take the photo out of the frame and see if there is any writing on the back that will solve this.

"We aren't going to. Put it back right where you found it. Let's focus on finding the key," Emerson centers me back to our original mission. Emerson continues shuffling through the desk drawers, and I stick my hands in a cardigan and a winter jacket. One has a ChapStick in it, and the other a wad of dirty tissues. Yuck. I would have taken Dr. Cramer as more of a "use a tissue, dispose of it in the trash, wash hands" type of guy. Not a "use a tissue, throw it in my pocket to allow ample bacteria to grow" type of guy. I should probably find a sink soon.

"Nothing. I can't find it." Emerson throws her hands up and sinks into his brown office chair. I think she's given up.

"Nothing for me as well," I say, trying hard to remember that whatever I touch next will be contaminated with whatever was on those tissues.

"Well, we tried. Let's get out of here before we get caught." Emerson runs for the door.

"You go ahead. I'll be right behind you," I tell her, but she has already scurried out of the office.

I take a seat in Dr. Cramer's brown swivel office chair. I spin around in circles. This helps me think. It matches the thoughts that regularly spin in my head. Finally, my body and mind are synced. I like this foreign land of "being one." So much so that I don't hear someone standing in front of the desk, watching me. If it's Ed, I'm not worried; he gets mad at me but eventually drops whatever it was when I make it up to him. Besides, he wasn't invited here, but then again, neither was I. But that doesn't stop me.

"Hello. What are you doing here?" Carl asks me. He speaks. This is the first time I have heard this man with a beautiful singing voice speak actual words!

"Oooops. I'm sorry. I'll leave. Please don't report me." I run out of the room faster than any drill Coach Morris ever made me complete at track practice. I bet she'd be impressed with my speed just now, especially since it's been months since I've trained and didn't even have a warm-up. I must have forgotten to include possible office cleaning services by Carl in my mission of picking Dr. Cramer's office lock to read the notes he writes about me during our sessions.

I slip into the recreational room, breathless. Emerson is in the corner playing solitaire with a deck of playing cards. She looks up and winks. If anyone asks me why I am out of breath, I must be prepared to convince them that this is what a panic attack looks like. Breathe. Breathe. Remember when Cole and I snuck into our parents' bedroom closet one December to search for unwrapped Christmas gifts? Remember how scared we were that we would be caught and only lumps of coal would be given to us? Which I thought was hilarious for my brother, Cole. But he was terrified.

He saw his requested Pokémon cards waiting for him to organize and trade. I saw my full set of *The Baby-Sitters Club* books that I was ready to read. I took one and snuck it back to my room. I read it under my covers with a flashlight at night. When I finished it, I put it back with the others and grabbed the next one. I did this until, five books in, the books were all wrapped and placed under the Christmas tree. I was annoyed.

I am annoyed. How could I have miscalculated the allotted time we had to pick that lock? I bet Mr. Klaus would be so disappointed in me if he knew. Maybe someone tried picking his lock, which resulted in it breaking. Whoever did this should have watched a tutorial and been patient the way that I had done with Dr. Cramer's lock.

"Lia, are you ready for your individual session with Dr. Cramer?" Nurse Wanda barges into my thoughts. She is consistent in doing so.

I want to warn her that Carl is in there cleaning the office, but I decide to stay silent and follow her down the hall. I don't want to draw attention to myself by knowing this since I was supposed to be in the recreation room with the others, not picking locks.

We pass the hallway bathroom. "Can I just stop here really quickly?" I plead.

Nurse Wanda nods her head and stands near the door. I pretend to pee by flushing the toilet and finally getting to wash my hands, which I have been waiting to do in a non-suspicious way since handling those tissues in Dr. Cramer's pocket.

"Thank you," I tell Nurse Wanda when I get out.

"Sure thing," she says as we walk each tile square closer to Dr. Cramer's office doorway. I cannot look. Is Carl still in there doing what he does best? Will he tell Nurse Wanda that he caught me in there without staff? I may never get to leave this place.

We arrive at room 217. The door is closed. Nurse Wanda knocks on it, then opens it when instructed to by a male voice inside. Whose is it? I couldn't hear with the preciseness that I needed to be able to identify whose voice it was.

"There you go. Have a good session," Nurse Wanda says, motioning me to walk into the office as she holds the door open for me.

"Lia, how are you?" Dr. Cramer asks, like his usual self. Nothing is different in his greeting. Perhaps he has not yet been informed of the incident.

"I'm okay," I lie. I really am more relieved than anything.

I glance at the fancy framed diplomas that are now slightly slanted. Has he noticed them yet?

"Lia, you know that this isn't a full feeling. I can bring out the feelings wheel if that would help."

"No, no, it's okay. I mean, I am feeling hopeful," I blurt out to avoid having that laminated wheel of colors and feelings being handed to me. I can't stand that. It makes me uncomfortable. It makes me consider many feelings that I did not even know existed but that I may have experienced and have no idea what to do with them. I'd rather stick with a few known terms.

"Can you share more? What are you hoping for?"

"Getting to level two soon. I have been doing everything the staff has been asking me to do. So, it should be happening soon, right?"

"Maybe," Dr. Cramer states, then sits in silence for a bit.

"Maybe" is a term I despise when I ask the gatekeeper whether the odds are on my side to leave this place and return to my previous life. It isn't convincing, and the silence that follows is torture. It's like having to anticipate the worst outcome or the best outcome and not knowing which it will be. It makes my skin crawl.

"Just tell me yes or no, Dr. Cramer. I can handle it," I plead for clarity.

"It depends," Dr. Cramer calmly states.

"It depends" might be even worse than "maybe." It feels like another teaser of a term to build the anticipation of having to experience the worst or best outcome later in the conversation. If anyone were to ever point a gun at me, I'd go crazy waiting to see what they decided. Will they pull the trigger or put the gun down? Just choose something fast, please.

"On what?" I continue to plead for clarity.

"On whether or not you think you are ready to dump Ed once and for all before leaving," he blatantly says. He has clarified things like I have been pleading for him to do, but now I wish I could sit in the "it depends" and "maybe" zones a little bit longer.

"Maybe," I state, then sit in silence for a bit. I amuse myself by staring at his slanted, framed diplomas and try to telekinetically get them neatly aligned. I don't believe in psychic abilities, so it won't work. I switch to silent prayer instead.

"Lia, what do you mean by 'maybe?' What do you think is holding you back?"

"Everyone and everything. The only one who was there with me when I went home last time was Ed. Everyone else had either left me, betrayed me, feared breaking me, or was too busy for me. But not Ed. We were tight."

"That makes sense why the thought of dumping Ed would be scary."

"I'm not scared. Not much scares me," I lie. I am scared that I will be caught for picking his lock and slanting his frames.

"You can be both brave and scared. You have overcome so much and have so much more to overcome. How was your outpatient team for support?"

"My what?"

"Your outpatient therapist, dietician, and psychiatrist. The referrals we discharged you with to continue your healing journey once you returned home."

"I didn't have those," I share, honestly. It feels so good to share honestly.

"Oh, no. That is a big issue. I'm sorry that those weren't followed through with for you. We need to be sure you have that when you are discharged this time. They are a team to support you not only in the transition home but also to help you learn how to live life without Ed."

"I can't really remember living life without him."

"I know. Can you imagine what your life could look like without Ed?"

"Sometimes, but then I feel sad. Like I'll end up all alone if Ed isn't there."

"Yes, I hear this a lot from others, Lia, who are making a big decision to leave a relationship that is not good for them. It is scary to imagine being alone. But I also know that once you dump Ed, you won't be alone. By breaking up, you are opening yourself up to other connections that Ed has kept you from. Do you believe this?"

"Sometimes. Recently, I've been feeling more alone with Ed, even when he's with me. It's like I don't really exist. I feel like he is the star of the show, and I am in the audience. Does that make sense?" I cannot believe I shared this. Dr. Cramer must think I need to stay here for many more months.

"Yes. It does. How about we agree to continue imagining life without Ed for the remainder of our sessions? How does that sound?"

"Scary, but I can try." I agree to his suggestion because, for the first time ever since meeting Ed, I felt a brief wave of relief when Dr. Cramer mentioned living without Ed—relief replacing my panic. I can start with this.

"Lia, are my frames crooked, or is it just my new bifocals?" Dr. Cramer asks as we head to his door.

"I think they are crooked." I am shocked at the words that come out. It's been fourteen days since entering these doors for the second time. Who am I becoming?

Chapter 25

"Good morning. It's Tuesday!" Nurse Wanda cheerfully calls out from my doorway.

"Good morning," I reply.

My trips from dreamland to reality have shortened. Sometimes, they happen within the blink of an eye. Or the opening of my eyes. This is new for me, but I like it.

Okay. Tuesday means treatment team time and tacos being served in the dining hall. Got it. This week, I am hoping to ask the treatment panel to consider leveling me up. Not in a Nintendo gaming system way, but in a finally getting to wear my hoodies and sweatpants again way.

I complete my morning ritual of changing my blue gown into a clean one, putting on my sock slippers, splashing my face with water, and joining the others in line at the nurses' station to wait for medications to be dispensed and cheeks to be checked. This place runs efficiently and rarely veers off schedule. It reminds me of living with my dad. When he was living at home, I could count on him being downstairs every morning, ready to greet my sleepy self in a cheery way. He had breakfast on the table, my heart plate at my seat, our lunches made and packed, and our backpacks lined up at the door.

"Lia, open up," Nurse Nancy requests of me.

I open my mouth as wide as I can and dangle my tongue. They like to check all parts of the mouth.

"Thank you, Lia. Your bite marks are barely visible. They are healing well," Nurse Nancy says with pride in her tone. I sense she is proud of me for not biting the inside of my cheeks as I had been. And so am I. Eating ketchup, marinara sauce, and oranges is a lot more tolerable now.

"Thank you. I'm trying." I walk away with a bit of a skip to my usual sock-skating. For the first time in a long time, I did something on my own which was not Ed-inspired. I feel proud of myself, and I am the star of the show for this one. It feels strange in this place, but also freeing, even when on a locked floor of a hospital.

"It was warm at night. I was cold as stone. But I still haven't found what I'm looking for. But I still haven't found what I'm looking for," Carl sings as he mops the tile floor of the hallway. I glance up, and he repeats, "But I still haven't found what I'm looking for." Is this a message about me searching Dr. Cramer's office the other day? Or is Carl just a big U2 fan? He seems to know all the lyrics to all their songs.

I smile and continue to sock-skate toward the group therapy room. I have got to keep things friendly with Carl. I cannot chance him telling the team about me inviting myself into Dr. Cramer's office without an invite. I'm most worried about having had access to contraband: the bobby pin. I got it from Nurse Wanda's bun, which sits on top of her head. She has many of them on her head each day—bobby pins of all sizes. One happened to be slipping, and I found the opportunity to take it. It really was an opportunity I had to take. It was too easy not to.

I choose a cold, hard chair in the group circle and face the others. This time, there is an empty seat in the circle where Christy normally sits. We don't have assigned seating, but we all tend to gravitate to the same chair each group, each day. We're reliable with each other and have created a system that seems to be working well.

"Let's get started, and Christy can join us when she is through with the treatment team," Nurse Nancy responds to the silent question, "Where's Christy?" that is occupying all our minds. I appreciate her ability to read a room.

"Today, I want us all to go around the circle and think of one relationship in your life that needs repairing. Let's start with Emerson."

"Okay. Um, one relationship that I'd like to work on is with my dad. I've been mad at him for the last couple of months because he moved us here from California when he got a new job. I have been rude to him because I've been mad. My new school is okay, and I have met some new friends, but I didn't want to move," Emerson shares.

Ah. This explains why I had not seen her around school at the beginning of the year. She's new to Woodside. She's new to New York. She's new to the East Coast. That's gotta be tough. I suddenly feel guilty for any ill feelings I had when I saw her at school that day with Ed.

"That sounds difficult, Emerson. A lot of changes at once. How do you think you can begin to repair things with him?" Nurse Nancy asks.

"Probably by beginning to believe him when he tells me how sorry he is to have had to move me during my freshman year of high school and how he had to take this job so that my mom wouldn't have to take on full-time work since he was being let go."

"That is a great step towards repairing. Who would like to go next? If no one volunteers, I'll call on someone."

"I'll go," I speak. I'd much rather take a proactive stance again and share on my terms rather than wait to be called on. Besides, it skips the whole awkward silence and the apprehension of whether it is me who is going to be called on next.

"Great. Thank you, Lia."

"I'd like to repair my relationship with Ed. It seems that Dr. Cramer and the others are encouraging me to end this relationship altogether. But I am wondering if I can repair it instead," I throw that out to the circle to chew on for a bit.

"Great question, Lia. How do you think you would begin repairing things with Ed?"

"I would begin by thanking him for all he has done by being there for me when others haven't been. I would then ask him to please allow me more space to be me- to lessen his opinions of me unless I ask him for them. To let me make decisions for myself instead of always thinking he is right and knows better than me. To tell me "good job" when I've tried hard at something instead of telling me I could've done better and do better next time. That kind of stuff."

"Great insight, Lia. Can anyone in the group identify with having had or being in a relationship like the one Lia describes?"

"Yes. It sounds awful, Lia. I'm going through something like this, and Dr. Cramer wants me to end it, and I finally want to, too. I tried to repair it before, and things were okay for a little bit. But it was only a matter of time before things returned to the way they were before the repair. In fact, they got worse," Christy says as she takes her seat in the circle.

"Lia, it's your turn with the treatment team. Sorry to interrupt your group, Nurse Nancy," Nurse Wanda says.

"Okay. Thank you, guys." I get up and follow Nurse Wanda to room 221.

As I enter the room, the treatment team panel is sitting at the table along with the gatekeeper himself. They smile and invite me to take a seat. Each week, it feels less and less like I'm being thrown to the lions. I take my seat at the table.

"Lia, we are so glad to have you join us today," Dr. J starts out the meeting.

"Thank you."

"We have been hearing from the staff out on the floor and from Dr. Cramer that you have been making some great progress in your treatment here," Dr. J. shares.

Should I consider this speaking behind my back about me, gossiping about me? Or not?

"We would like to hear your thoughts on how things have been for you here since your return," Dr. J asks.

Did he really have to remind me that this isn't my first time here?

"I think I am making progress. I still have lots to work on." I find it hard to toot my own horn, unlike Cole, who does it on the regular.

"Yes, I agree, Lia. As you know, the work must continue after discharge. It sounds like you didn't have a support team to meet with when you went home last. Do you know why this is?" Dr. J asks.

"No, but I can imagine my mom didn't think it was necessary. She threw me a party when I got home last time and continued sending the message to me that now that I am out of the hospital, I am cured, healed, and fixed."

"Yes, unfortunately, this occurs with some parents, which is why we try so hard to teach them what real healing will require and how they can best be a part of this journey with you."

"I don't think she wants to do it anymore. I get the feeling that I'm just more work for her and that I need to figure this out on my own."

"I'm sure that isn't the case, Lia. Many times…"

"It is the case this time, Dr. J." Dr. Cramer interrupts to conclude my hypothesis.

"I've spent multiple sessions with Lia's mother and many phone calls. It appears she is just not able to do what Lia needs to heal at home, currently. This does not mean things won't change at some point. But this is what I have observed for now."

"Well, then, thank you for this, Dr. Cramer and Lia. I suppose the next step in treatment is to explore other support systems outside of your mother for now. How do you feel about moving on to level two at the end of this week?"

"I feel excited! Thank you!" I smile. I didn't even need the feeling wheel for this one.

"Great. Then I will get started on the paperwork on this end, and you continue to do all the hard work that you have been doing on your end. Keep up the great work, Lia."

Wow, he congratulated me without me being perfect.

"Lia, let me walk you back to the group room," Nurse Wanda says.

"Emerson, your turn for the treatment team," Nurse Wanda says as I scooch back into my cold, hard chair.

"Welcome back, Lia. How about we continue exploring with the group if repairing things with Ed is an option or if it would be better to dump Ed? Is that okay? I know we didn't have a chance for you to finish processing with the group before being called out to the treatment team."

"I guess so." I can't risk not complying and no longer leveling up at the end of the week.

"Great. Can anyone in the group share with Lia about a relationship they had tried to repair, but the other person wasn't willing to do their part to change to support the other? Or where the relationship ended, and how you coped with the ending?" Nurse Nancy throws out the questions to the other members of the group.

Please, can someone say something soon?

"I've been dumped before. It did not feel good," Theo says, saving me from the tense silence.

"Me, too," says Max. "Eventually, I began to feel better. Until I saw her at school with someone new."

Oh, great. This sounds reassuring. I wish Dr. Cramer were here to hear these testimonials straight from others my age. I must ask…

"Do you think it's because they dumped you instead of you dumping them?" I must assess how my proactiveness can help me if I decide to listen to Dr. Cramer's recommendations.

"I think they are both difficult to experience, Lia. But perhaps being the one to end the relationship may feel differently than the other way around," Emerson adds.

"I think it helps with time once you can 'get your life back' from your ex," Max says.

"I am scared that I won't be able to get through things on my own without Ed," I admit to the group.

"That makes sense, Lia. Untangling from Ed can be scary. But you have already been doing this while you've been here, and you are safe and okay," Nurse Nancy reassures me.

"I remember how scared I was to be alone again after I dumped my ex. I forgot what I liked when I was with him," Emerson adds.

"I get that. At first, I thought being with Ed was exciting, but it turns out that he makes me forget who I am—who I was before we met." I am just unraveling here. I glance at the clock, and it looks like I am saved by the bell!

"Well, it's time to wrap up the group. Thank you everyone for sharing today. I encourage you all to take this to your individual therapists to discuss further. Let's line up for morning snack."

Chapter 26

"Good morning! See you down at the station in five!" Nurse Ron chants out. I hear him say the same to each doorway down the hall of Hoodie Heaven.

I arrived late last night. The treatment team panel kept their end of the deal and leveled me up, just like they said they would. It is taking some getting used to, believing that others are going to do what they say. It's weird, but I like it. I splash my face with cold water and brush my teeth. We are allowed to have some of our personal items on this floor, and it feels good to be reunited with my tube of Colgate.

After throwing on a new hoodie and sweatpants, folding the others, and placing them under my plastic-covered pillow, I quickly make my bed and head to the nurses' station for medication rounds.

"Lia, here you are," Nurse Ron hands over my small plastic cup of medications and a small red solo cup filled with water. I take them, then thank him as I hand him back the empty cups. He disposes of them in the recycling bin. We skip the whole "cheeking" routine on this floor. Apparently, we are growing in our recovery, and they increase our independence to allow for a smoother transition to leaving. For them, independence is defined as switching out our sock slippers for slip-on shoes. Switching out blue hospital gowns for our own tie-free sweats. Switching out the spork at mealtimes for a fork and a spoon. I have other definitions for it.

I head to the recreation room where we are supposed to gather before breakfast. We can choose to do a puzzle, look out the window and dream of being free, or play a game with one of our peers. I glance around the room, but everyone is new to me. No familiar faces. Why does this feel like a version of having to walk into the school cafeteria and wonder where I should sit? I walk toward the window. I can see the parking lot filling up quickly with patients, staff, visitors, and whoever is making their way to the hospital today. Others are leaving the parking lot and getting their day started elsewhere.

Part of me wishes I could be part of the world happening out there. Another part of me doesn't feel ready. I've gotten used to things here, and I like knowing what comes next.

"Hi, I'm Vicky. Do you want to play Connect Four until it's time for breakfast?" A blonde girl around my age dressed in violet sweats asks me.

It's not fair if I immediately dislike this girl named Vicky because she is dressed in violet, the name of the mean girl Chloe has replaced me with as her new best friend.

"Sure. I'm Lia." I decide to take the higher ground.

"Cool," she says as we take our seats at the round table and set up the game.

"Is it okay if I'm red? I am mad about having to have a family session with my mom, and red is anger on the feeling wheel Dr. Cramer shows me at each session. It's fine if I'm not," Vicky asks.

"He shows you that wheel every time, too? No problem; you can be red." We both chuckle together.

"Thanks."

"Sorry, you have to have a session with your mom today. I'd be mad, too." I stack a black checker onto one of her red ones.

"Yeah, she's just now trying to be a mom to me when she hasn't been since I was born. It's kind of late to start now, when I'm in high school, you know?" Vicky starts a new row when placing her red checker. I think I see what she's planning to do to get four red ones in a row.

"Yeah, I get it. Dr. Cramer stopped doing sessions with my mom because we did them the last time I was here, and when I went home, she didn't make any of the changes. Sometimes, I wonder if she even cares about me at all, you know?" I might just win this round. Her strategy is good, but I've mastered this game with hours upon hours playing against my dad when I was younger.

"Yeah. I tend to think that about my mom, too. Wait a minute. You were here before?"

"Yeah. A couple of months ago," I embarrassingly admit.

"Cool. So, can you tell me something about Nurse Ron? How old is he?" Vicky smirks while she asks.

"Are you serious? Not you, too. Some of the girls who were here the last time thought the same thing about him. Sorry, but I've got no information on the guy. His lips about his personal life are sealed," I say as I stack my fourth black checker in a diagonal row. Game over.

"Lia, can you come meet with me now? I will be sure to have your breakfast delivered to my office," Dr. Cramer says just as the game ends. His timing is impeccable.

"Okay," I lie. I'd much rather eat in the dining room with the others than in his office.

"Great. Follow me," he invites me to follow him down the tiled hallway, into the elevator, and upstairs to his office, room 217.

"Good morning, Carl. How are you?" Dr. Cramer asks as we walk into his office.

"Good morning. I'll be out of your way," Carl says as he grabs his dusting equipment and leaves Dr. Cramer's office. I smile at him and hold my breath. Please don't mention when I picked the lock of this office. I cannot return to this floor and trade out my sweats for a blue gown AGAIN. Or my fork and spoon for a spork AGAIN.

Carl closes the door behind him, and Dr. Cramer invites me to take a seat. He is already holding his yellow legal pad and red pen and sitting in his brown swivel chair. I grab a seat on the couch and glance at the fancy framed diplomas, which are no longer slanted but are neatly aligned once again. Evidence has been destroyed. I thank my lucky stars.

"Lia, thank you for meeting with me. It looks like you are getting settled in level two. Making some new friends."

"Yeah. Vicky seems cool."

"Good. You know, a big part of your recovery is going to be building new connections with others who are not Ed. How do you feel about this?"

"You don't need to bring out the feelings wheel, Dr. Cramer. I basically have it tattooed on my brain. I'm feeling excited and scared about this."

"That is normal. The thought of meeting new people and letting go of others can be scary. I'd like to remind you how much you have already done that while you've been here. Can you see this?"

"I guess. It just feels easy to do here because I know what things are like here. Does that make sense?"

"It sure does. Here, we offer you structure, routine, stability, and a staff that is invested in your healing. I know you have been missing those things at home with all the changes happening there."

"Yeah, I suppose. It just stinks that I'm the one who must leave everything and come here when it feels like I'm not the only one at home who has issues to work on!"

"I know this is hard. That is why we have been working on how you can remain empowered to continue healing during their issues without trying to fix things for them or have their actions affect you negatively. Having an outpatient treatment team for support when you leave will be extremely vital."

"Okay. I'd like that because I don't have anyone at home that I can talk to."

"Not even Ed?"

"Not really. Lately, he is so stubborn. He thinks I am wrong, and he is right. If I don't do what he wants me to do, he makes me feel guilty. Then, I must make it up to him to make things better. This happens over and over. I don't even know who I am anymore," I confess for the first time to myself and someone else.

Knock, knock. Nurse Wanda hands me my breakfast tray. She smiles and does not speak, then turns around and leaves the office. Eggs, ham, toast with butter, oranges, and milk. I miss my coffee.

"Go ahead and get started, Lia. I will grab mine and eat with you," Dr. Cramer says as he gets up from his chair, grabs a brown paper bag, and takes out a large New York onion bagel with cream cheese and lox piled on. He grabs his cup of coffee, which smells delicious.

"Hey, thanks for eating with me. It makes it easier than having you just stare at me. That's what my mom does. Depending on her diet of the week, she skips meals and rarely sits with me. Cole is so busy eating with his friends at their houses, it can feel lonely. Ed constantly complains about what we're eating, so he's no fun to eat with anymore."

"Of course! Meals are an amazing way to connect with others. Please disregard the lox smell. I'm sorry if it bothers you at all."

"Nope. But your coffee smells delish!"

"How do you normally drink your coffee? I love sugar and creamer," he says as he takes a long swig of his coffee.

"I used to like mine with the limited-edition flavored coffee creamers, but then Ed started telling me it's better to drink my coffee without all that stuff. So, I stopped and just drank it plain." Another surprising confession to myself and another person.

"I'm sorry. How about you promise me that if I give you a day pass for this weekend to go home, you will drink your coffee with your favorite flavored creamer? And if Ed is there and begins to give his unsolicited opinion, you tell him to back off and get lost!"

"Really? You think it's possible for me to get a pass home already?" I ask with a mouthful of eggs, not caring what is revealing itself right now from my mouth.

"I don't see why not. I will have to get the rest of the treatment team members to sign off on it, but I don't think that will be an issue if you promise to give this homework assignment a try. Deal?" he asks, eagerly waiting for an answer.

"Yes!" I confidently reply. There is no chance I'm going to let Ed ruin this for me.

"Great! How about we spend the next half of our session preparing a plan for if Ed, Cole, Chloe, your mom, your dad, or anybody else you see on your pass can't support you in completing this homework? We can prepare you with a plan to support yourself through this. You are very strong, Lia, and I know you can do this. You can even call in to our staff here if needed."

"Sure. I really want to be more independent; I just need to trust myself again."

"That makes sense. Being in a relationship with Ed where your thoughts, feelings, and actions are constantly being questioned and doubted, you can begin to really doubt yourself and trust his perspective over your own."

"Yes. How can I begin to be me again?"

"You are already doing it. The more you spend time with other people instead of Ed, and the more you practice using your voice instead of Ed speaking for you, the more you will be you."

"So, kind of like the group we had the other day where I had to identify which was my thought and which was his. It was tough at first because they both kind of became one. But as I detangled them, I was able to see more of which thoughts are mine and which are his."

"Exactly! Keep working on that and bring them into session next time, will you? I'd like to see your list."

"Sure." How am I not even hesitating to share my and Ed's innermost thoughts with someone else? Ed will be furious. Maybe because I finally feel like I have backup again. Like I did when my dad still lived at home.

Chapter 27

"Okay, Lia. You know the drill. I'll walk you to the front of the hospital, and your brother and father will be there to pick you up for your day pass today. Once you get back, Nurse Wanda will come downstairs to do a contraband search and process how your pass went. Any questions?" Nurse Ron asks.

"Nope. Not my first time doing this," I reply embarrassingly.

"Lia, you do know that we have many patients who come back to treatment, right? You are not the only one. Each time, they learn something different about themselves, their lives, a new skill, etc. We are not a one-and-done place," he compassionately explains to me while witnessing my embarrassment.

"No, I guess I haven't met the others who have been here before, too."

"Well, you will after you are discharged. In the alumni group that meets here on Wednesday nights. All of us on staff take a turn running it each week, and it's pretty cool seeing how far everyone has come since leaving and giving support to those who need it."

How did I not know this was an option when I left the first time? I bet my mom knew about it but was so busy with work and Phillip that she never considered bringing me!

"Okay, here they are. Have a great pass!" Nurse Ron says as we stand outside, watching my dad and Cole pull up to the curb in Cole's red Jeep. Nurse Ron holds the door open as I climb in and buckle my seat belt. When I'm all settled in, he closes the door and waves. The people here really do take good care of us.

"Hi, honey! I am so glad I get to spend the day with you," my dad says as he turns towards the back seat and gives me a big smile.

"You are free! Well, at least for the next seven hours. What do you want to do?" Cole playfully jokes around with my freedom, and I do not find this funny.

"Oh, come on, Lia. I'm just poking fun at you," Cole defends himself to my disappointed and serious face.

"Okay. Are you and Chloe still poking fun at me by being together behind my back and making me look like an idiot by not telling me that my big brother and best friend—ex-best friend— are dating?!" I blurt out. Man, that feels good. I've been holding it in for so long, listening to Ed telling me to keep the peace and not stick my nose in other peoples' business. But I am not listening to him anymore, at least during this day pass. I am supposed to listen to myself and use my voice. Why not get started on it right away?

"Geez, Lia. You couldn't even wait until we left the hospital parking lot before bringing this up?" Cole tries to stall from answering me.

"No, Cole. I couldn't. I have known for months and have kept my mouth shut, but no more. Tell me why. Why did you have to get with my best friend? Sometimes, I think we have so much in common, but at times like these, you remind me of our mom and how selfish she can be. At the very least, Chloe should have told me!"

Again, this feels good. Getting all my words out that I have been swallowing for so long. I imagine I could work on my emotional regulation or volume some, but I'll get there.

"I'm sorry, Lia. I should have told you. Mom made me promise not to. She said you may relapse and that you are too fragile to know about it."

"You listened to Mom? She doesn't know me the way I know myself. I would have rather you both had told me. I don't get it. Why does our family keep so many secrets? Did you know Mom is getting serious with that veterinarian?" I feel betrayed. I don't need a feeling wheel to help me with this one.

"I did. Again, she told me not to tell you," Cole admits.

"Of course you did. Of course she did. Do you know how crazy it is to have so many secrets under one roof, Cole?"

"Well, technically, you aren't currently under the same roof."

"Are you serious right now?! Please drop me and Dad off at this coffee shop up here on the right," I beg while waving my finger to where I must immediately escape.

"Good idea. I can go for a coffee right now, too," Cole says as he pulls into the shopping center where the Cup of Joe shop sits. Luckily, it looks open.

"Okay, let's all get out and take a breather," my dad finally intervenes.

Cole pulls into a parking spot. We get out. I slam the door harder than I should have, but I am aware of this. And awareness is the first step to changing, but I'm not interested in changing my door-slamming behavior right now.

"Welcome. What can I get you?" a boy with an eyebrow and nose piercing who looks to be my age asks. He has a blue streak in his hair. I am not sure if it is hair chalk or the real deal, hair dye.

"Hmmm, I'll try an Americano, please," my dad gets us started on the orders.

"I'll take a large latte." Cole jumps ahead of me in line to order. Of course, he does.

"I'll just take a black coffee," I state.

"Are you sure? We have so many different drinks to choose from," The blue-streaked hair, pierced boy behind the counter asks.

"Yes, I'm sure," I confidently say.

"Okay. That will be four dollars and twenty-five cents. And tips are always welcome," he says, smiling and pointing to his tip jar on the counter.

"Here's a tip…what's your name?" I blurt out.

"Ed. My name is Ed. Nice to meet you," he says and smiles.

You've got to be kidding me.

"Okay, Ed. Here's a tip for you. The next time someone who is working on building their self-esteem and using their voice orders a drink, don't suggest that they doubt their decision, okay? Let them choose for themselves. Got it?" I strongly suggest.

"Sure. No problem. Sorry, I'm new, and the manager gave me this to say when someone orders the cheapest drink on the menu. I'm supposed to try and encourage you to purchase a specialty drink so this place can continue staying open with profits," he explains to me.

"Okay," I say and immediately take a seat.

"You need to chill, Lia. Maybe you should have ordered a relaxing tea instead of caffeine," Cole says as he walks to the men's restroom.

My dad and I take a seat at the wooden table. The legs are a bit uneven because it wobbles back and forth whenever I lean my elbows on it. Am I being too loud? Too much? Should I tone it down? I know Ed would tell me to—not this coffee shop Ed, but my Ed.

My dad looks concerned now that I've placed my order. I know what this is about.

"Um, Ed, do you have any special edition holiday creamers?" I ask from my rocking table.

"The store doesn't sell it; it takes away the upselling to the specialty drinks. But I've got my personal stash in the back that I brought from home. It's sugar cookie. You want some?" he asks.

How is he even thinking of sharing something with me after all I have said?

"Sure. That would be great, thank you," I say across the empty shop.

I tap my fingers on the table.

"Here you go: one coffee with some sugar cookie creamer and one large latte," Ed says as he sets the cups down on the wobbly table.

"Thank you," I say as I bring the creamy white cup of coffee to my mouth. I smell the sweetness of the creamer. I am scared to take a sip. I don't know if I can handle feeling so wrong and bad for drinking it because Ed doesn't like me to.

I take a quick chug and swallow it fast, barely even tasting it. If I am going to drink it, I should drink it fast. Maybe Ed won't notice?

"Why don't we take it to go and get back on the road home?" Cole says when he arrives at the table. I hope he washed his hands.

"I'd rather stay here; I want to speak with Dad for a bit. Then you can take off," I speak what I want again without so much hesitation this time.

"Sure. Whatever you want," Cole is supporting me.

"Thanks," I take a warm sip of my creamy white sugar cookie-flavored coffee. I fall in love with it immediately, remembering the joy these creamers used to bring me.

"Let's not wait too long, Dad. I know you have a lot more packing to do for your move." Cole drops an emotional bomb at my feet as he takes a seat at the table with us.

"Dad, you're moving? To where?" I can barely spit out, as I feel like I am gasping for air.

"To Chicago. I took that new position I told you about," my dad calmly states.

How is he so calm about this? I know Ed is going to tell me bad things happen when I do bad things, and this is my penance for consuming the creamer.

"Dad? Are you for real?" I ask robotically. I feel like I am observing my life as an outsider.

"Yes, Lia. I have been wanting to tell you. Dr. Cramer suggested I do it when I see you in person next, not over the phone."

I hope Dr. Cramer knows what he is doing by recommending my father tell me something in person instead of over the phone.

"Cool. I'm glad that you guys are able to talk. I'm going to hang out in the car and listen to some music while you do so," Cole says, standing up and finishing his latte.

I want to leave, too, but if I stand up, I might fall. Breathe. Breathe. Breathe. I take a sip of my coffee and then breathe as if Nurse Nancy is leading a relaxation group. I name five things I can see. My white creamy coffee. The wooden table. The boy behind the counter. The trash can. The jukebox in the corner. I name four things I can touch. My sweatpants. My warm yellow coffee mug. The rough tabletop. The curves of my fingernails. I name three things I can hear. The grinding of the coffee beans. The song "I Can't Get No Satisfaction" playing on the jukebox. And the ringing of the bell when a new customer walks into the store. I name two things I can smell. The sweetness of my sugar cookie creamer. And the scent of a familiar cologne. I name one thing I can taste. My delicious cup of coffee with creamer. I take a big sip. It tastes amazing.

I look around me. I am no longer floating above and looking into my life. I am here, in it.

"Lia, I'm sorry it took me so long to tell you," my dad says.

"When were you going to tell me?" I harshly ask.

"I wanted to tell you sooner, but I had to wait until I spoke with your treatment team, your mom, and Cole. You know, to get it all sorted out." I sense he has more to say. So, I sit in silence. This has been becoming easier to do since being in treatment. Breathe.

"It turns out Chicago is a big city," he goes on, pointing out the obvious. I remain silent and listen. "And I was given some names of providers in the city that Dr. Cramer recommends—providers that he wants you to see when you leave the hospital," he continues. "I spoke to your mom and Cole, and they are supportive of this."

"Of what, dad? Supportive of what? I am tired of being the last person in this family to find things out."

"To move to Chicago with me, Lia. Would you like to?" he asks.

I cannot believe this is happening. I don't know what to say. Part of me does not want to leave New York; I barely had a chance to be at Woodside High. But another part of me can't imagine having my dad so far away again.

"You don't have to give me an answer now. I know it's a lot to take in," he says.

"YES! I will move with you, Dad." I jump up and hug him. We stand in the coffee shop, hugging to the song "Stand by Me" playing on the jukebox. Is this real life?

Chapter 28

"Good morning, Lia. How are you feeling?" Dr. Cramer asks me at the start off our last session together, which means this is the last time I will see him swiveling in his brown office chair.

"A bit sad, but also excited," I declare after considering a variety of feelings from the memorized feelings wheel.

"That is to be expected. How do you want to spend your last session before discharging today?" he asks as he holds his yellow legal pad and red pen.

"I'm not sure," I admit. A few ideas cross my mind, like, "Let's review those scribblings you keep of me on the yellow sheets of paper that are locked up in the filing case." Or beg him to share one personal detail after having heard thousands of mine over the course of months.

"How about we start by discussing where you are with saying your goodbyes to the staff and other patients here? Have you begun to do so?"

"Not really. For all we know, I might end up right back here again. Maybe I should forget the goodbyes and tell them, 'See you later?'"

"I think it's best if you commit to saying your goodbyes this time, Lia. Things are different this time around. You will have your outpatient treatment team meetings at least twice a week to start with. You can attend our alumni group weekly via Zoom. You are supported this time. Your dad has already forwarded me this week's dinner ideas, as well as the days and times of your upcoming appointments. He even spoke to your new school counselor so you can have lunch with them while you begin to meet friends there."

"I know. I just don't want to jinx it. I thought last time would be my last time here, and I was wrong."

"You are right. And I want to remind you how far you have come since then. Last time, you wouldn't even entertain the idea of dumping Ed. This time, you actually did!"

"Wait, so you knew I was not ready to dump Ed last time? How did you know? I didn't tell you."

"Because, Lia. I have been in this field a long time. I know when someone is ready to dump someone and when someone is telling me what I want to hear in order to be discharged."

"Oh. Well, I guess I should tell you…" I am not brave enough to finish my sentence.

"What? That you broke into my office one evening, and Carl found you in here? Yeah, he told me."

"What? How come you never said anything? How come I still leveled up that week?"

"Because, Lia. Your persistence and creativity in going after something once you set your mind to it is a gift. Do not lose that. Just be aware of when Ed tries to use this gift of yours to trick you into thinking you are doing something because it'll help you when really it is hurting you. But you know this. You now know again who you are. And that will continue to grow as you meet with your new team in Chicago," he shares.

I know he is right. Since using my voice and talking back to Ed when he tries to make me feel bad about something that I don't need to be feeling bad about, I've been feeling more like myself and stronger each day. Even though I did dump Ed, it doesn't mean that he's completely gone just yet. I know one day soon he will be. But for now, I remind myself that our run-ins will continue to happen. And I know these will be less and less over time until he's gone for good.

"You've got this, Lia. Stay in touch," Dr. Cramer says.

"Thank you. I will."

"Let's head over to your closing circle before your dad comes to pick you up," Dr. Cramer says as he walks us to the hallway.

Breathe. Breathe.

The End

LEADER RESOURCES

As an educator, mentor, coach, or parent, you play a pivotal role in the lives of young athletes and students. You are often the first to notice the subtle changes in behavior, mood, and performance that may signal underlying challenges, such as disordered eating or the early stages of an eating disorder. These guides are designed to equip you with the knowledge and tools needed to recognize these warning signs, engage in meaningful discussions, and take appropriate action. By fostering a supportive environment and intervening early, you can make a significant difference in the health, well-being, and future of the young people in your care.

COACH MORRIS'S GUIDE TO RECOGNIZING EATING DISORDERS IN ATHLETES

"As coaches and trainers, we play a crucial role in the lives of young athletes and are often the first to notice changes in their mood, behavior, and performance. These changes may signal disordered eating or an eating disorder. Early detection is one of the best predictors of full recovery. By promptly involving the athlete's parents or guardians in discussions, we can take the necessary steps to address these issues. It's vital that we take any warning signs seriously—cardiac arrest and suicide are the leading causes of death among those with eating disorders," Coach Morris emphasizes.

"I've included some scenarios from this past season, along with suggestions on how to handle them. Remember, always make a prompt referral to a medical provider and involve the athlete's parents or guardians."

Scenario 1: Increased Training Without Nutritional Support
Lia abruptly increases her running mileage but does not adjust her nutritional intake accordingly. Additionally, she is stressed from receiving lower-than-average grades in Mr. Klaus's class. She eventually suffers a tibia stress fracture, which is discovered in the emergency room.

Response: Changes in routine and stressors at home or school can significantly impact an athlete. As coaches and trainers, we should talk to new team members about the challenges they may face during the season and offer healthy coping strategies. Enlisting the school counselor, like Ms. Amy, can help reduce the risk of unhealthy behaviors such as restrictive eating or excessive exercise. Additionally, it's essential to gradually increase running mileage during the preseason and encourage parents and students to make appropriate nutritional adjustments. A registered dietician can be a valuable resource in these situations.

Scenario 2: Missing Menstrual Cycle You overhear Lia telling a teammate that she has never gotten her menstrual cycle.

Response: This is a red flag that warrants a referral for medical evaluation. If the cause is medical, it can be managed by a doctor or referred to a specialist. If delayed menstruation is due to extreme exercise or disordered eating, the athlete should be referred to a registered dietitian and an eating disorder therapist.

Scenario 3: Unhealthy Training Habits A teammate asks Lia how she can become a better athlete, specifically how to train like Lia to win races.

Response: While it's important to nurture motivation in young athletes, we must also be vigilant about the potential for some to take training to unhealthy extremes. This behavior could indicate the early stages of an eating disorder. Do not dismiss this as simply being perfectionistic. Look for other signs, such as overuse injuries, training beyond what's recommended, exercising in dangerous conditions, high anxiety when unable to train, frequent weighing, negative comments about body shape or weight, and muscle weakness.

To foster a healthier environment, it's crucial to eliminate negative messages about weight, size, appearance, and dieting from the team culture. Avoid public weigh-ins or doing them in the presence of other students. In fact, consider eliminating weigh-in policies altogether unless absolutely necessary.

As coaches and trainers, we must also be mindful of our own attitudes and behaviors regarding food and exercise. It's important that we do not model a disordered relationship with either. If we need support in this area, we should have the courage to seek professional help.

MR. KLAUS'S GUIDE TO DISCUSSING DUMPED WITH STUDENTS (A TEACHER'S GUIDE)

For High School Students

"Remember, fellow teachers, it's helpful to begin by asking students what they understand about the topic being discussed. By engaging their perspective, students will feel more invested in the discussion because it shows that you value and respect their insights and opinions," Mr. Klaus advises.

"Ms. Amy, our school counselor, teaches that eating disorders are complex medical and psychiatric illnesses. Even if a student doesn't meet the full diagnostic criteria for an eating disorder, the consequences of disordered eating can be severe and long-lasting, requiring intervention. Early intervention can prevent the progression to a full-blown clinical eating disorder."

Pre-Reading Activities:

- **Reading Journal**: As you read each chapter, keep a journal to record your reactions and feelings about the characters and events. Include any predictions or conclusions you might draw as the story unfolds.

Writing Activity:

- **Persuasive Paragraph**: Write a persuasive paragraph discussing whether you think Lia should or should not be allowed to read Dr. Cramer's notes on her.

Discussion Questions:

1. **Chloe and Ms. Amy**: Why do you think Chloe confided in Ms. Amy about her concerns regarding Lia's relationship with Ed? What does this tell us about Chloe's character?

2. **Lia's Ritual**: Why do you think Lia relied on her favorite plate to start each day? What might this ritual signify?

3. **Lia as a Typical Teenager**: In what ways is Lia a typical teenager? How is she similar to or different from you?

4. **Mr. Klaus**: According to Lia, what was unusual about Mr. Klaus? Does Mr. Klaus remind you of any teachers in your school?

5. **Lia's Anxiety**: Why does Lia think about times with her dad when she feels anxious? What does this reveal about her relationship with him?

6. **Author's Purpose**: What do you think the author's purpose was in writing this book? What key message or idea was she trying to convey?

Teachable Topics:

- **Dieting and Adolescents**: Is dieting a normal part of adolescent behavior? While concerns about body image and dieting have become common in teenage life, dieting can be a risk factor for developing an eating disorder, especially for those with family histories of eating disorders, depression, anxiety, or obsessive-compulsive disorder. Emphasizing overall well-being and self-acceptance is a healthier approach.

DR. CRAMER'S GUIDE FOR PARENTS OF A TEEN STRUGGLING WITH AN EATING DISORDER

As a parent, discovering that your teen is struggling with an eating disorder can be overwhelming and frightening. You may feel a mix of emotions—worry, confusion, guilt, or helplessness. It's important to remember that you are not alone, and there are steps you can take to support your teen during this challenging time. This guide is designed to help you navigate difficult conversations with your teen, understand the underlying issues, and provide the support they need to begin the journey toward recovery.

1. Starting the Conversation

- **Choose the Right Time and Place:** Find a quiet, private moment where you can talk without interruptions. Ensure that both you and your teen are in a calm state of mind.

- **Express Concern Without Blame:** Start the conversation with "I" statements to avoid sounding accusatory. For example, "I've noticed you seem stressed lately, and I'm concerned about how you're feeling."

- **Be Prepared to Listen:** Allow your teen to express their feelings and thoughts without interruption. Show empathy and understanding, even if what they say is hard to hear.

- **Avoid Criticism:** Steer clear of comments about their appearance, weight, or eating habits that could be interpreted as judgmental. Focus on their emotional well-being instead.

2. Understanding the Underlying Issues

- **Acknowledge the Complexity:** Eating disorders are *not* just about food or weight; they stem from deeper emotional issues such as anxiety and depression.

- **Explore Triggers:** Gently ask your teen if there are specific situations or feelings that make them want to restrict food, overeat, excessively exercise, or engage in other disordered behaviors.

- **Recognize the Role of Perfectionism:** Many teens with eating disorders struggle with perfectionism in their lives. Understanding this can help you approach the issue with more empathy.

3. Offering Support

- **Encourage Professional Help:** Eating disorders are serious medical conditions that often require professional treatment. Encourage your teen to see a doctor, therapist, and dietitian who specializes in eating disorders.

- **Reassure Them of Your Love and Support:** Let your teen know that you are there for them, no matter what. Remind them that they are valued and loved for who they are.

- **Set a Positive Example:** Model a non-disordered relationship between food and body image in your own life. Avoid making negative comments about your own or others' appearances. Avoid dieting behaviors and excessive exercise.

- **Establish a Supportive Home Environment:** Create a home atmosphere that promotes "all foods fit" eating without judging foods. Refrain from dieting and excessive exercise behaviors in the home. Focus on family meals as a time for connection. Avoid talking about food at the table. Instead, engage in light table topic discussions.

4. Navigating Difficult Emotions

- **Be Patient:** Recovery from an eating disorder is a long process, and there will be ups and downs. Stay patient and avoid expressing frustration or disappointment.
- **Validate Their Feelings:** Even if you don't fully understand what your teen is going through, it's important to validate their emotions. Statements like "I can see this is really hard for you" can be very supportive.
- **Encourage Open Communication:** Let your teen know that they can come to you whenever they need to talk. Keep the lines of communication open, even if the conversations are difficult.

5. Involving the Family

- **Educate the Family:** Make sure that everyone in the household understands the basics of eating disorders and how to support the teen in recovery.
- **Promote a Positive Body Image:** Encourage all family members to talk positively about their bodies and avoid negative self-talk or comments about others' bodies.
- **Encourage Shared Activities:** Engage in activities that promote well-being and connection, such as family game nights, watching movies, or other hobbies that your teen enjoys.

6. Seeking External Support

- **Join a Support Group:** Consider joining a support group for parents of teens with eating disorders. Sharing experiences with others who understand can be incredibly helpful.

- **Work with the School:** Collaborate with your teen's school to ensure they receive the necessary support during this time. This might include adjustments to their schedule, extra time for assignments, or access to counseling services.

7. Moving Forward

- **Celebrate Small Victories:** Recovery is a gradual process. Celebrate your teen's small steps forward, whether it's attending a therapy session or trying a new food.

- **Stay Hopeful:** Maintain hope for your teen's recovery. Remind yourself and your teen that with time, support, and professional help, recovery is possible.

- **Keep Learning:** Continue to educate yourself about eating disorders and recovery. The more you know, the better equipped you'll be to support your teen.

ADDITIONAL RESOURCES

If you or someone you know is in need of help,
please don't hesitate to reach out.
Support is available to everyone.

National Eating Disorder Association
ANAD
National Alliance for Eating Disorders